Touching Bass

By: Lynn Leite

This is a work of fiction. Names, characters, places and incidents are the product of the author's imagination or are used fictitiously, and any resemblance to actual persons living or dead events or locals is purely coincidental.

1

The phone was somewhere. Baylor just couldn't remember where she had put it down. Eventually, the person calling would give up, but Baylor worried it might be an emergency.

The ringing stopped. "It's probably someone trying to tell me my warrantee has expired," she said to herself.

When the ringing started again, she went into full panic mode. What if this was an emergency? Her family didn't live close by or call often. It could be another solicitor or spam, but her gut was telling her it wasn't. Baylor always listened to her instincts. Some might call her freaky, but she just knew sometimes. This time, she knew that the ringing phone was important.

"Hello," she said as she dove for the phone when she located it.

"Hi Bay, guess what?" Her best friend's tone didn't spell disaster or even concern.

"Maren, did you just call me?"

"Yes, you didn't answer, so I tried again. I have great news."

"Good, I was worried."

"You are always worried. This is spectacular news. Get ready for the night of your life. I'm picking you up in an hour."

"No, you're not." Baylor wasn't convinced that her sense of foreboding wasn't still active. Just because the phone call seemed like a happy one didn't mean her gut was wrong. She wasn't in the mood for one of Maren's fun evenings.

Maren's definition of evening fun was usually fun and innocent, but something about her gut thinking the phone was bad news still made Baylor cautious.

"You have to com., I need you. The most amazing thing happened."

"You met a guy?" It was a good guess considering Maren met a lot of guys who would like more than just the bubbly friendship she offered.

"No, I won a contest."

"A contest?"

"Yes, you know that Rascal is in town. Since they grew up around here, they are doing their last night of the tour at the Arena." Rascal was a local band that had made it big.

"I did hear that." Baylor saw where this was going. This was what she had sensed might ruin her night. She hated loud concerts where people were packed in like sardines. She didn't dislike the music. She just preferred a sound she could turn down if it was too loud.

"I won two VIP tickets. We will be up front. So close that Austin Day will probably sweat on us."

"That's disgusting."

"Oh, you know what I mean."

"I do and it also puts *you,* not *us,* right next to the speakers."

"I have ear plugs. Just get dressed. I'm coming in a half hour."

"Tonight?"

"Yes, tonight is the last night. They are going back to the studio and I heard that Sydney is pregnant."

"Sydney?"

"Austin's wife, you know Stacy."

"I thought you said her name was Sydney."

"It is the song. "Stacy" and "Obsession" were written by him for her before she even knew he was more than a friend."

"Aren't we a little old for Boy bands?"

"How dare you? Rascal is a re-emergence of Classic rock. They have a European tour in the works."

"Alright, they aren't a boy band."

"Please come with me? I need you."

"You need me?"

"Yes, I might embarrass myself and throw myself at one of them and only one is even single. You ground me."

"I had a feeling when the phone rang that I wasn't going to like the message it brought."

"I need a wing man."

"You *need* to stop fangirling."

"Did I mention the tickets were free and VIP? We get to meet the band."

"Yes, along with ten or fifteen other fanatics."

"It's once in a lifetime. I could never afford to see them and the more famous they get the more the tickets sky rocket."

Baylor couldn't argue with Maren's logic. Maren and Baylor both just made ends meet. A ticket to a show of this caliber was out of their price range. Two free tickets shouldn't be snubbed at.

"Alright, I'll go."

"I knew it. I promise you'll love the show."

"Right, sweaty Rock stars and screaming fans. Just bring those ear plugs. I like their music but not enough to risk going deaf."

By the time Maren arrived, Baylor was glad she had said yes. This was a once in a lifetime thing. The kind of event she would probably tell her children about. Lord knew she had heard her father's story about how he almost went to Woodstock, enough to know he regretted not going.

"No regrets," she said to the mirror. Her feeling of doom was more a 'Proceed With Caution' sign now.

Her gut churned for an entirely different reason. She was excited. Not like Maren, who would probably scream louder than the music the entire time. Baylor was nowhere near the level of Maren's obsession. She was, however, a fan of their music and might even be able to sing along with a few.

"You're wearing that?" Maren said with her hands on her hips as soon as Baylor opened the door.

"What's wrong with this?" Baylor had a semi-tight pair of jeans on with a lace tank and a pair of flats.

"It's fine, I guess," Maren said, tilting her head to the side. It's just plain.

"You mean unlike your see-through top with a red bra underneath it?"

"If you've got it, flaunt it."

"I'm at full flaunt on an hour's notice."

"You're right. You're gorgeous all the time. Maybe, take the hair down?" Maren said shyly.

"It's going to be hot in the Arena with all of those people."

"But we will be up front, right where the cameras are."

"Maren Elizabeth, what are you talking about, what cameras?"

"They might be filming the concert."

"Might be or they are?"

"They are, but the band, not us, unless they pan the crowd."

"What have you gotten me into?"

"You will be fine. You look amazing. Let's just go. The limo is waiting."

"Limo, what limo?"

"The Radio station sent it. It's part of the prize."

"Is there anything else you forgot to mention?"

"No, that's it."

Baylor was hopeful that the rest of the night was uneventful. She already had enough surprises.

2

"Could you please not do that in front of me?" Joey yelled, covering his eyes. His sister, Finley, who was officially part of the Rascal team, was wrapped around the drummer in a way that no brother should have to see.

"We were alone when we started," Griff laughed.

"Fine, maybe be a little more discreet."

"You're just mad I took your wing man," Finley said, righting herself and turning to her brother.

"I do fine on my own."

"Like with Yasmine?" Finley mentioned the Security female that was hired after the last tour.

"She had a crush on me. Turns out we were not really compatible."

"In other words, she dumped your ass," Griff nodded.

"It was mutual. You a can ask her."

"I did. She said it was mutual. I give you credit for being mature about it, both of you," Finley complimented." You're growing up, Little Brother."

"Yas is great. We are good friends now."

"See, old Joey would have been angry or hurt."

"Old Joey wouldn't have tried a real relationship at all. With all of you hooked-up or married and having kids, I am the last man standing."

"We are still standing. We just have support. Come on, it's showtime," Austin called, having heard the last part of the conversation.

Griff and Joey exchanged a look before joining Austin." You know your sister just wants to see you happy," Griff said.

"I am happy. Yas is seeing one of the roadies and I am happy for her. I am single and ready to mingle. You're still shacking up with my sister. When are you going to make an honest woman of out of her?"

"It's not 1950, Joey. I asked her to marry me."

"You did?"

"Yes, I did."

"And she said no?"

"She said yes. We were going to mention it later. We have six months off and I might need a Best man."

"But you'll settle for Joey," Austin taunted.

The four band members that made up the band Rascal were like brothers. More than brothers, in a way, since they spent more time with each other than most brothers would.

"Very funny."

"Finley isn't big on the idea of a big, fancy wedding. I'm letting her handle it," Griff grinned.

"That's what I did. I just showed up," Austin joked. They all knew he helped arrange his wife's dream wedding. Despite a helicopter crash, a tropical storm, and a daring rescue, it was a beautiful ceremony.

"Are we ready?" Race called, seeing the others approach. Mark, their manager, and Teagan, Race's soon to be wife, handed the four of them a shot.

It was a tradition to toast to Hank before every show.

Hank was Sydney's Dad and the man that gave the band their first break. The not old enough to be in a bar band had been hired by Syd's Dad to play weekly. The local fame and then world-wide fame that came after might not have been possible if Hank hadn't bent the rules and let four teens with a dream play in his place.

"To Hank," they said, downing the mild shots and grabbing their instruments as the lights came up on the empty stage.

"Contest winners are down front. Make sure to play to them. The cameras are on," Mark instructed.

"Should I crowd surf?" Race joked.

"No, absolutely not, Rufus would have a stroke," Mark laughed. Rufus was Head of their personal security, a giant of a man with an imposing demeanor that was the opposite of his true nature.

"If Rufus had a stroke, then Aunt Olivia would tell Teagan and I'd be in big trouble."

"Is Teagan's Aunt still seeing Rufus?" Joey asked.

"They are moving in together. Teagan thinks they are secretly married," Race shook his head. Olivia looked like a Wood spirit that dressed in flowing layers and Rufus looked like he could eat you for breakfast.

"Good for Rufus," Joey said as Austin took the lead and they went on stage.

The roar of the crowd and the warmth of the lights never got old. Joey felt it every time he took the stage. They all did, that electric connection to a thousand or more people who had come to hear what they had to offer.

They were going on a break to go back into the studio and make another album. It would be months before they took the stage again. He was going to miss this.

Scanning the front couple of rows, he saw the group of VIPs. Old Joey would be picking out the blonde with the see-through shirt as someone to get to know. She was bouncing and screaming as they started to play.

New, Joey felt empty with that kind of disconnection. He didn't know that girl and objectifying her was wrong. Of the five or six beautiful women in the first few rows, he had only noticed her because she was wearing practically nothing. He wanted something real. Yas had been a good start. He had been telling the truth. The break-up, if you could call it that, was mutual. When it came down to it, he and Yasmine were better friends than lovers.

The music flowed. His fingers knew the chords. He could play most of their songs in his sleep. This was his passion. His life was the music and he had the good fortune to be able to do this for a living.

Joey focused on playing to the VIPs. Making eye contact made the fans feel special. It also was good for the video. Being the last single band member, the flirting and suggestive looks were now solely up to him.

As soon as he tore his gaze from the blonde's chest, he noticed the beauty beside her. The woman was smiling, not screaming like some of the other women. She looked like the girl next door. Her body swayed slightly as the music seemed to fill her. She was listening, really listening. She wasn't looking at the stage. She had her eyes closed, lost in the moment. Out of all of the people Joey could see past the glare of the stage lights, she stood out.

Willing her to open her eyes, Joey's focus was on her and her alone. The blonde next to her nudged her with an elbow and pointed up at him. As soon as she realized he was looking at her, she stopped swaying.

Joey felt her eyes on him as a smile bloomed across his face. Then, the moment was gone. She looked down at her feet, shaking her head saying something to the blonde that he wished he could hear.

3

"He's staring at you."

"Who?" Baylor looked up to the stage and saw that one of the band members was looking in their direction.

"See, he's looking right at you," Maren yelled to her over the sound. Even her ear plugs didn't block out Maren's excitement.

She was right. The Bass player was looking right at her. He could have been looking at Maren with her fire engine red bra, but Baylor swore she could feel his eyes on her. It was too much. She had to look away or get lost in the eyes of a man who was way out of her league. Baylor didn't even know which one he was. For all she knew, he could have been the married one.

"He's working the crowd," she said, looking away from the stage.

"He was looking right at you."

"Or he was looking at your lack of clothing."

"I'm going to ask him when we go backstage."

"Oh no, you are not. I'm not even going backstage. You're on your own."

"Would you two shut up!" A large angry woman behind them growled in between songs.

"Excuse me?" Maren looked at the women like she was dirt. Maren had a way of making people do what she wanted them to, but she also had a rough childhood in some sketchy neighborhoods, where backing down showed weakness.

"I said shut up!"

"Look, I doubt our voices were louder than the music, but we will keep it down," Baylor stepped in before Maren did something stupid.

"Look, Sweetheart, some of us paid for these tickets and they weren't cheap. Just because you have some lame pass hanging around your neck so you can pretend you have a chance with any of them doesn't give you the right to ruin my night. He wasn't looking at you anyway."

The woman wasn't dropping it and Maren had fire in her eyes. Even the Security guys were watching the show in the front rows.

"We will keep it down. Maren, you don't want to get kicked out, do you?" Baylor hissed. "I knew I shouldn't come out tonight."

"I'm fine. We are fine, all good," Maren insisted, turning back to the stage as Rascal started their second set.

Now, the eyes on her were coming from the security on either side of the stage.

The crowd was on their feet and the general admission crowd behind them were closing in. The larger-boned woman with the attitude was purposely shoving at Baylor's chair, so the metal of the folding chair hit the back of her legs just below her knee.

Baylor took a step forward and the chair followed.

"Enough, get over it. What is your issue?" Baylor lost it for a second before turning back to watch the rest of the show trying to ignore the woman.

The shove from behind was unexpected and a lot stronger than Baylor would have thought.

Falling forward, trying to get her legs under her before she could face plant, she managed to stumble right into the stage's edge, taking the Security rope and the poles holding it with her.

Her forehead slammed onto the lip of the stage and she crumbled in a heap. She turned back toward where she had been expecting another attack. It was just in time to see Maren rushing toward her and the big girl behind them being grabbed by Security.

"Are you alright?" the voice she heard first wasn't Maren. She was having trouble focusing, but the voice was distinctively male.

"What did you say?"

"Someone go get Finley," the voice called and Baylor felt herself being lifted and then moving.

"Oh my god, Bay. I'm so sorry," Maren said from somewhere behind her.

"Bring her too," another male voice barked, this one terrifyingly firm.

"I knew I wasn't supposed to come out tonight," Baylor said more to herself than anyone else. From now on, she was going to listen to her gut when it says a life-changing event is about to happen. The head injury she was sure she had wasn't really all that life-changing, but the embarrassment of the moment would last forever.

"I'm glad you did come out tonight," the male carrying her was serious.

"Then, you must be an asshole," she groaned

"I've been called worse."

"Oh god, it's Joey White." Maren's voice was a shrill, stabbing sound that Baylor was sure made her brain bleed. "Baylor, it's Joey White."

"Stop talking, Maren, I'm going to throw up."

"I've got you," the male said, turning her so she was facing away as a trash can was offered by one of the other people there.

As she puked into the small trash bin, she realized that the music had stopped. She was backstage. That much she knew. The man who had carried her there had placed her on a very nice couch. She couldn't think straight or she might have wondered what took place on this couch after a show. She had heard the rumors.

"I'm so sorry," Maren whispered.

"It's my fault. I should have listened to my intuition and stayed home."

"This will be one hell of a story someday. Let me take a look at your head," a gorgeous woman said while pushing her way through the crowd and staring at her.

"A real show stopper," Baylor quipped, wincing at the woman's touch.

"I would say so. I'm Doctor White. You can call me Finley. "

"Finley White, in person?" Maren squealed.

"You apparently have a fan," Baylor groaned. Her head was killing her and the noise felt like shards of glass in her brain. "Maren, can you please keep it to like a one on the Fangirl scale?"

"Sorry, she's Griff Williams' girlfriend and Joey White's sister, am I right?"

"Yes," The Doctor laughed.

"I'm not sure who any of those people are, but I'll take your word for it."

"You don't know who anyone is?" the Doctor asked with concern.

"Maren is the fangirl. I am the wing man. I know I'm at a Rascal concert. I know I got pushed by a very scary woman with an attitude. I don't know all the band members by name or instrument like Maren, and I don't keep up with the rumors about them."

"How many fingers?" The Doc said smiling.

"A lot, my head hurts when I try to focus."

"You hit it pretty hard. You have a nice gash on your head that needs stitches. I can do it here, but I'm no Plastic surgeon."

"Where is it?" Baylor reached up, touching the spot where it hurt and regretting it immediately.

"It's near the hairline, but you are bleeding a lot. Someone get her a shirt she can wear."

"She looks like Carrie at the prom," Maren called.

"Thanks, Maren, I love you too," Baylor groaned.

"You boys better go finish the show. I've got her," Doc Finley said, making Baylor realize the band, the managers, and half the Security force was crammed into the little room they were in.

"I really did stop the show?" Baylor laughed, looking from blurry face to blurry face.

"Technically, Joey jumping off the stage was what stopped the show." She knew the man answering her was the Lead singer. He had a very distinctive voice.

"Joey White?" she said, remembering what Maren had been so excited about.

"At your service."

"Go finish the set, Hero. I will keep you posted on how she's doing," The Female Doctor chuckled.

"You're in good hands. Finley is the best," Joey said, sending shivers down her spine. She might not be able to see much, but she was sure this was the man that had been staring at her from the stage.

4

Baylor declined the offer of an ambulance and took the offered ride from the Manager, his wife, and Joey White's sister. Maren was filling her in on who was who, despite the fact that Baylor hadn't asked.

Joey White, the Bass player, had apparently jumped off the stage, throwing his guitar in the process. He then rushed to carry her off *Wedding night* style.

Maren had always been a great storyteller.

Since it was all a literal blur to Baylor, she just listened.

"All sound stopped. The big screen showed you being carried by Joey and the guards taking Shenna off in handcuffs."

"Sheena?" Baylor looked at Maren, who was turned around in the front seat of the SUV and, somehow, she still had the seatbelt on.

"She looked like a Sheena, or maybe a Bertha," Maren shrugged.

"She's being held on Assault charges." Mark, the band's Manager, called back as he drove.

"Maybe, she was just having a bad day," Baylor started to say.

"Oh no, she pushed you hard and the world saw it. She shoved that chair into your legs and you said nothing. She deserves what she gets. You can't go putting your hands on people like that. She was rude and out of line and you were too nice to her," Maren said with a finality that Baylor heard.

"Do you know what her problem was?" Amber, who was Mark the Manager's wife and the one that was in charge of publicity, asked.

"She didn't like that I was telling Baylor that I thought Joey was staring at her. She told us to shut up, so I said 'What the hell?'. Baylor is a peacekeeper. She runs a quiet bookstore on the edge of town. I didn't want to make trouble and let that go. I should have punched her," Maren talked so quickly it made Baylor dizzy.

"Then, you'd be in jail instead of Gretchen," Baylor pointed out.

"Gretchen, I like that one. So, anyway, Olga starts spewing that she paid her ticket and we got in for free because we were VIP women who would sell ourselves to get a shot at the band."

"She said that?" Finley asked.

"Not those exact words, but it was implied. We stopped talking and ignored her while she moved Baylor's chair closer and closer until Bay had to step forward. Bay yelled at her and went back to staring at Joey."

"I was not staring at Joey."

"Fine, I was. Then, Helga shoved her with both hands and Bay flew into the stage. You know the rest," Maren smiled.

"I'm sorry you missed your Meet and Greet," Baylor whispered as they all five entered the Emergency room.

"Are you kidding me? I met all of them. I'm hanging with Joey's sister and the band's manager right now. Other than you needing stitches, this is amazing."

"Only you could put a good spin on this disaster of an evening."

"It's all how you look at it."

"I'd listen to her. She's right." Finley waved at the woman behind the desk and they went right in.

"See, Finley White agrees with me. She saved people from a crashed helicopter at Austin and Sydney's wedding."

"I'm really going to have to pay more attention to the tabloids," Baylor looked at Finley.

"The tabloids are not always right. Maren is correct. There was a helicopter crash at the wedding, because the tabloids wanted a story bad enough to fly in a tropical storm."

"It sounds like it was a good thing you were there. I am glad you were there tonight too. I'd be waiting out in the Waiting room for at least five hours if you weren't."

"I have hospital privilege here. I'll call a good friend who is an excellent Plastic surgeon to do the stitches. She won't leave a trace."

"I don't mind a small scar. I'm no supermodel."

"Even covered with blood in a tee-shirt two sizes too big, we can all see that you're stunning," Finley, who was actually stunning, insisted.

"Thank you."

"So, are you really a Bookstore owner?"

"It might seem stupid in this digital age but yes. It's small and I do a lot of Online business. I make my living dealing in rare and antique books. People still buy paperbacks, mostly romances and mysteries."

"I love a good romance," Amber, the Publicist, said, looking up from her phone. "Baylor, I think we need to talk about a few things."

"I'm not going to sue, if that's what you're worried about."

"No, I wasn't worried about that. I'm worried about you and your health. This has gone beyond the incident itself. What happened has already hit the news feeds."

"Meaning?"

"Meaning that hundreds of Rascal fans had their cell phones out."

"Great, now I'm a GIF flying into the stage over and over while gushing blood. Am I right?"

"Yes and no, I did see one showing the moment you hit your head. The others are Joey jumping off the stage and carrying you off."

"That's about Joey, not me."

"You would think, but here's what's trending: #Joeys' girl, #Romeo, #Love at first sight."

"That's mostly focused on him."

"There's more," Amber said softly.

"More? It's been an hour."

"Welcome to your fifteen minutes of fame," Maren teased while looking at her own phone. "'*Who's that girl?' 'When did Joey start dating for real? 'Seems like a set up', 'I wish he looked at me that way.*'" Maren gave Baylor an I told you so look before resuming her scrolling. "'*Another one bites the dust', 'What's she got that I don't?'*... you get the gist."

"All because a guy came to the rescue of a girl in trouble?" Baylor's head was starting to clear and it was not looking like the stitches would be the end of this.

"All because a Rock star, a public figure, a single public figure, stopped in the middle of a show being filmed to carry you off the Arena floor." Amber put her spin on it and made it a much bigger deal in the process.

"So, now what?"

"Now, we need a statement."

"Like what? Thanks for the save, Joey."

"That's not too bad. The fans are already speculating that you two are more."

"More what? I didn't know him before. I still don't. I'm sure he's a nice person. He'd have to be to save a perfect stranger from being pummeled by Agnes."

"I liked Helga better," Maren smiled as they all sat in a room, waiting for Finley's Surgeon friend. She was clearly enjoying the idea of Baylor's fifteen minutes of fame.

"Fine, Helga, Inga, Doris, whoever it was doesn't matter. The point is I don't know Joey. I didn't even know which one was Joey until Maren told me."

"We can put that in your statement, but it will look like you are trying to hide something."

"Like what? I'm not hiding anything. There isn't anything to hide."

5

Teagan was waiting for the men as they left the stage after their second encore. “The remaining contest winners are waiting. The report from the hospital is that the woman is fine and Finley is making sure she gets the best care. Joey is trending along with the mystery girl.”

“Trending?” Joey asked.

“You tossed your bass, jumped off the stage, and carried a woman off the Arena floor.”

“She was hurt.”

“I’m not saying you were wrong. I’m saying that you had a cell phone wielding audience,” Teagan smiled.

“My hero,” Race cried in a high-pitched woman’s voice as he hugged his bandmate.

“Cut it out, she needed help. You said she’s okay?”

"I said Finley is with her. She has a concussion, a mild one, and she's waiting for a Plastic surgeon to stitch up her forehead."

"What happened to the woman that attacked her?"

"Did you say she attacked the woman, Joey?" Teagan tilted her head, waiting for an answer.

"I saw the whole thing. She was slowly pushing the woman's chair forward. The woman and her friend were trying to ignore her. I was looking right at them when the larger woman behind them shoved the woman in front with both hands, knocking her off balance and sending her into the stage."

"You saw all of that?"

"Yes."

"He was staring at the woman long before the incident," Race added.

"Please, tell me you were not scoping out the VIPs? I thought we were past that," Teagan was only partially teasing.

"I'm past that. I wasn't looking at her like she was a groupie that I could take advantage of, if that's what you are insinuating. If anything, her friend would have been an easier target. She just caught my eye. I was interested, not going to lie."

"I was mostly joking, Joey. You have matured since we first met."

"Do I need to remind you that you met Race when you came back after a show?"

"I was at the show because Amber offered me a job, but you are right. I'll talk to Rufus, but we might need you to make a statement to the police."

"After the VIPs, I'd like to go to the hospital." Joey would have liked to go to the hospital right then but knew that they had an obligation to fulfill. Checking on a woman he didn't even know was not an excuse to bail on his bandmates.

"If she's still there, I'd say yes but check with Amber. You checking on the woman is good press, but it could be the wrong message to send. I can't make that call."

"I will check with Amber first."

"We should probably all go, so Joey doesn't look like a stalker," Griff taunted.

"I was just hoping to get to know a woman I was attracted to. That's not stalking."

"Enough, go, shake hands, sign a few things. I will check with Amber about going to see the woman."

"Can you find out her name, so I can call her something other than the woman?"

"He wants her name. This might be serious," Austin laughed.

"Says a guy that spent years loving his best friend before he finally admitted it," Joey reminded.

"Leave him alone, maybe she's the one?" Teagan said sarcastically. "The internet already thinks they are dating. "

"Last week, you and Race were on the rocks, according to the internet." Joey wasn't wrong. The rumor mill and the paparazzi got almost as much wrong as they did right.

"The price of fame," Teagan smiled, letting the men into the room filled with eager fans.

Normally, Joey loved this part. In the past, all four of the Band members might find a willing bed partner in the group. That was then. Now, three of them were either married or engaged. Even Joey's sister was wearing a ring. Griff and Finley hadn't made the announcement official, but Joey knew his sister and one of his best friends were in a forever relationship.

Joey didn't feel left out exactly, but he did feel like he had outgrown the one-night stands and indecent offers. He wanted to settle down one day, have kids. Austin and Sydney were already expecting their first. They weren't kids playing in a garage anymore.

The fans, as usual, were thrilled to meet them. Joey would never get used to the fact that thousands of people, maybe millions, knew him by name. Tonight was different. He wanted it over with. He wanted to go see the woman that had captured his attention before she was hurt.

"Alright, there is a car waiting out back. Austin and Sydney already went ahead."

"Is she alright?"

"She's going to see the injured fan. She's fine. She's pregnant, not sick."

"Right," Austin nodded.

"Whatever happened with the woman that pushed her?" Joey still didn't have a name. He had heard her friend say it but he hadn't really been paying attention. The woman was covered with blood. Joey knew from experience that head wounds nearly always looked worse than they were.

"She is under arrest for assault," Teagan answered."

"The woman pressed charges?"

"Not yet, even if she doesn't, we have hundreds of witnesses, a lot of videos, and she bit Rufus."

"She bit Rufus?" they all said in unison.

"On the wrist, he's been seen at the hospital, but the woman who bit him… let's just say she's having a very bad night."

"Rufus should get checked for rabies. What the hell was wrong with that woman? Were there drugs involved?"

"I couldn't say, but I'm sure they will test her. She assaulted two people, made a scene, and resisted arrest."

"Miss Teagan, we have a problem," the driver said as they took a turn onto the street the hospital was on.

"What problem... oh... go around back."

Joey leaned forward to see what was going on. The front of the hospital came into view and so did at least seventy young people, mostly woman.

"Does that sign say I wish I was Joey's girl?" Race laughed as they passed.

"Yes, I'm calling Amber." Teagan held up a finger as she called the Manager's wife to see how to handle this potential PR nightmare.

6

"Hold on," the woman who was Rascal's press person rushed to the window. They were in a room on the fourth floor of the hospital in the Maternity ward. Amber had thought that would be the last place the press would look for Baylor.

At first, Baylor and Maren had thought that it was a gross exaggeration. They were sure the Press would focus on Joey and the band, not Baylor. The back halls and service elevators seemed like overkill. The band wasn't even with them.

"What is it?" Maren said, standing to look. "No way! Are they here looking for us?"

"Who is they?" Baylor asked, standing up too quickly and getting dizzy.

"Woah, Girl, take it easy," Sydney steadied her as she sat back down.

The Lead Singer's wife, Sydney, introduced herself when she arrived and Maren acted like she was the Rock star, not just her husband.

"You have to stay still or this will look worse than if Finley did it," the woman who had joined them said as she wiped Baylor's forehead.

"Always the comedian," Finley groaned. "What's going on out there?" she asked, turning to Amber and Maren.

"A crowd is outside the front entrance," Maren explained in a flat tone.

"They probably assume that the guys are here. Even if you weren't rumored to be Joey's girl, they would come to check on you," Amber explained.

"I am no one's girl."

"We know that, but the perception of the audience is that he acted like you were special to him."

"He *was* staring at you," Maren chimed in.

"Or he was staring at your red bra, the one you can clearly see through your see-through shirt. When can I go home?"

“We will see what we can do about getting you out of here as soon as you finish being stitched up. You will need to be observed for a few hours because of your injury. Concussions can be tricky. As long as you have someone that can stay with you tonight. Do you need anything for pain?” Finley looked at her colleague, who had arrived to do the stitches in her head.

“Maybe something, but I don’t want to be out of it.”

“I’m using a local anesthetic for now,” the woman who came to stich her up said. “Now, lie back and we will get started on stitching you up. You have to remain as still as possible.”

“Right here, right now,” Maren squealed.

“She’s squeamish,” Baylor explained.

“Then, don’t look,” the Doctor said, making it sound like an order.

Baylor nearly hit the roof when the Doc stuck the first needle in to numb the area, but the rest wasn’t bad at all.

As soon as she was done, they handed her a mirror.

Twenty tiny neat stitches above her left eye were barely visible.

“Nice work, how long until I can take them out?”

"Four or five days," the Doctor finished saying and the door opened, startling all of them.

The four men and one woman that came into the thankfully large Maternity suite were familiar. Maren's silent scream as she slapped her hand over her mouth while swaying on her feet confirmed that these men were the same four that had been on stage hours before.

One man, in particular, felt strangely familiar. He was staring again, focused on her forehead.

"Best... day... ever," Maren said slowly.

"Are you serious? We are at the hospital and I have a head injury."

"Bay, we are at the hospital with Rascal and Sydney, Finley, and Teagan are hanging out with us."

"I'm lost. I know this is Finley and Sydney introduced herself when she arrived. I assume you are Teagan."

"Process of elimination."

"Teagan is Race's fiancé. Finley and Griff are a thing as well. You know Sydney and Austin's story," Maren sat hard on the bed, jostling Baylor.

"Watch it," she winced, raising her hand to touch her head.

“Don’t touch. Let me bandage it,” the Doc ordered, pulling Baylor’s hand away.

“Hi, I’m Joey.” Baylor glanced up at the man’s face and felt a surge of emotion.

“I’m Baylor, thanks for the save.”

“I’d say it was my pleasure, but you scared the hell out of me. I saw that woman push you.”

“I didn’t see that coming at all, and to think I almost stayed home,” Baylor glared at Maren.

“You didn’t want to come to the show?”

“No offense, I just had a feeling that something might go wrong.”

“Like a premonition?” Joey sounded like he was truly interested. He wasn’t judging her like most people did.

“You could say that.”

“So, if you tell me not to get on a plane, I shouldn’t go.” Joey’s smile was lethal. No wonder Maren had nearly lost her mind when he carried her off the floor.

“If anyone said not to get on a plane, you shouldn’t go,” Finley chuckled.

“Baylor almost didn’t come with me. I had to drag her out of the house. Now, I feel like I should have listened. My name is Maren. It’s so amazing meeting you all."

Baylor smiled at her friend and regretted the facial movement. Maren had toned down the rabid fangirl and was acting more like herself at the moment.

"Our Grandmother had a weird Sixth sense," Joey looked to his sister for confirmation.

"You could call it that. She was eerily right about some things, but I would call it more woman's intuition combined with the wisdom of age," Finley agreed.

"Mine is more paranoia than anything. I just felt like going out tonight might not be the best idea."

"And now look at you," Maren was back to mild fangirl mode. "You're hanging with Rascal and their significant others. Can I get a picture?"

"Sure," Amber said when all eyes went to her.

"Your optimism astounds me at times," Baylor sighed.

"You have to admit this is a once in a lifetime experience," Maren looked apologetic.

"I hope so. You're right. We are hanging with people that most of those at the Arena would kill to hang with. From my point of view, I was nearly knocked out. I bled all over my favorite shirt. I threw up on the drummer."

"I play bass," Joey grinned, thoroughly enjoying this woman's rant.

"Sorry, I threw up on the Bass player. I'm hiding in a Maternity ward suite because I'm rumored to be dating said Bass player and there's a GIF of me hitting my head over and over going viral."

7

The more time he spent in Baylor's presence, the more attractive she became to him. She was real. She wasn't trying to impress any of them. Even describing her night was more like a comedy routine than a complaint.

Joey didn't realize he had reached out to take the woman's hand until he had it firmly in his. Baylor looked at him with a questioning glance but didn't pull away.

"Bay, you're going to laugh at this someday," Maren, her friend, said with her eyes glued to her phone.

"What are you looking at now?" Baylor reached out to grab the phone with her free hand.

Joey leaned in as the GIF of Baylor hitting the stage head first played on repeat with accompanying sound to go with it.

Maren was waiting for Baylor's reaction and Joey was assuming that tears would come.

Baylor smiled weakly then chuckled at the GIF. "You're right. Someday, this will be hysterical."

"There's another," Maren smiled. This one was Joey jumping from the stage in slow motion, his bass flying back, nearly hitting the drums.

"You look like a superhero. Thank you," Baylor turned to him.

"He's lucky he didn't break an ankle," Finley scolded in a teasing tone.

Baylor was starting to see that these people were more than a band. They were family.

"Alright, I have good news and bad news," Amber addressed the group.

"Bad news first," Baylor said before anyone else could respond.

"Alright, the bad news is that the police are here and we have no safe exit at the moment. I'm working on a plan, but it doesn't look like you're going home anytime soon."

"Are the police here because of the people outside?"

"They are here to speak with Baylor mainly. Maren and Joey were obviously witnesses to the assault. They will want to speak to you as well."

"What's the good news.?"

"The good news is that you don't have to go to the station to make a statement. The hospital is providing a private room for tonight, since Finley said you need to be observed. Oh, and I'm going to need to speak to the two of you about how to spin this with the media."

Amber looked to where Joey was sitting on the bed with Baylor, her hand in his. The moment Amber looked their way, Baylor pulled her hand away.

"Spin this?" Baylor asked. "There is nothing to spin. A crazed woman shoved a fan and, seeing the attack, Joey jumped down to help."

"I think you both need to see some of the footage that's surfacing online. Even I am not buying that you two never met before and I know it's the truth."

"What does that mean?" Baylor asked, leaning away from the man beside her.

"Oh please, I told you he was looking at you."

"So what? Even if he was looking at me and not you in that half bathing suit you are wearing, we were in the front row."

"People's imaginations can build an entire relationship from a look like this," Amber clicked on a still shot where Joey looked like he was starving and she was cake.

"I was and am still extremely attracted to you," Joey added, not caring that the room was full of all of his friends and family.

"I am flattered, but..."

"But what, are you married, seeing someone?"

"She's single. Baylor, don't be stupid." Maren was back to bouncing on her toes, ready to go full fangirl again.

"Stupid would be saying I was his girl when it's a lie. Isn't it recommended that you not make big decisions with a concussion."

"She is right. Even thinking about this probably hurts," Finley looked like she was enjoying the show.

"Joey, I'm sure you're a great guy."

"I get it. I'm not your type."

"Showstopping, woman rescuing men are everyone's type. I just don't see this as working for real and I'm not going to lie for a Publicity stunt. I'm sorry."

"Don't be sorry. Amber, is there any mention of her name anywhere?" Joey asked.

"No, so far, she's just the Mystery girl. It's just a matter of time."

"Can I speak to Baylor alone?" Joey asked the group.

"Five minutes, we are moving to another room where the police can take your statements. I'll be outside," Mark gestured for the others to leave.

"Bay?" Maren looked sad.

"I'll be fine. If you need to go home, you can. I'm in good hands here."

"I'm not leaving you."

"Go, I'll be right there."

Baylor's stomach knotted as soon as they were alone.

"We should go," she said, looking at Joey. He was nice to look at. His voice did things to her lady parts and his eyes were speaking to her. She didn't want to fall into the dating trap with a man that could walk out the door and have ten offers of no strings attached sex.

"No not yet, why don't you think that you and I would work in real life?"

"Because you are you and I am me."

"That is a non-answer, Baylor. I'm a man who is interested in you. If you're not interested in me, then just say so."

"That's not it."

"Good, so go out with me sometime: dinner, coffee, on a date or just as friends, you choose."

"I can't help but think this conversation is only happening because the media already thinks there is more going on."

"I was interested before all of the media."

"You were interested in a girl you saw in the front row. How many front row girls have you been with?"

"A lot."

"Thank you for being honest."

"I wasn't interested in them for more than a night. You are different."

"I'd like to believe that, but I'm not taking the risk. Sorry, it's still no."

"Can't blame a guy for trying?"

"You can't blame a girl for wanting more than just a fleeting moment with a Rock god."

"Rock god?"

"Maren's words, not mine."

"Can we at least exchange numbers? I really would like to check-up on you, maybe talk you into coffee."

"Yes, here, put your number in," Baylor handed Joey her phone after unlocking it.

"Don't sell it."

"If I wanted to cash in on my fifteen minutes of fame, I'd date you, Joey." Baylor wasn't going to admit that she was tempted to take him up on his offer. Not because he was a member of a famous band, but because he seemed so genuine.

"The fact that you are not cashing in just makes you even more attractive to me."

8

"Great, so the two of you have decided that dating for real was a no go. We still need to tell the press something," Amber had hoped they would act on the mutual attraction they had for each other.

"Tell them the truth. I found a woman I wanted to know in the audience and she got hurt. I acted on instinct. Say I was just doing what Finley would have," Joey said, knowing the media had eaten up the story of Finley saving the reporter and Helicopter pilot.

"I was going to suggest fake dating," Maren smiled.

"Fake dating, Maren?"

"Happens all the time. A prince wants the king to get off his back, so he fake-dates a maid or something."

"What the hell are you reading?" Baylor laughed.

"Or like Trevor, you get a girlfriend for another reason."

"Who is Trevor?" Joey asked, liking the fake-dating story. It would give him time to get to know Baylor, maybe even convince her to really date him.

"Trevor is a friend from High school. He is gay. His parents didn't know so he had a girlfriend all through High school. She knew he was gay. Everyone did." Baylor rolled her eyes, then winced because the action hurt her head.

"She agreed to be his fake girlfriend and she was Best woman at his wedding last year when he finally came out," Maren explained.

"Before we go further, I would rather remain a mystery. Fake-dating him would just cramp his style and make me look like an ass."

"I wouldn't cheat on you."

"It's not cheating if I'm not really your girl."

"Then, be my girl."

"Just because the world made an assumption? That's a terrible reason to ask a girl out."

"I really want to date you, Baylor."

"Oh my god, Baylor, if you don't, I will."

"Maren, I think the offer might be exclusive. Tell you what, Joey, if in a week or two, when the media forgets all about this because some other celebrity sneezed or something, then you can call me."

"And you'll go out with me?"

"I'm pretty sure that weeks from now you'll have moved on but sure, coffee sounds innocent enough."

"We are going with the truth then?" Amber sounded like that wasn't the plan she was hoping for.

"Yes," Baylor looked away from Joey. As much as she would like to think that he was genuinely interested, she couldn't help but think he was temporarily interested and saying yes to him would make an already bad evening worse.

After another hour of telling the police what happened, Baylor was done. After making a call to her Assistant, telling her to open the store in the morning. Baylor settled into the private room provided. Her head still hurt and she was exhausted. All but Amber and Maren had left.

"I'm not going to say it," Maren said softly.

"Good, because my head hurts," Baylor knew that Maren thought she had done the wrong thing turning Joey down.

Baylor was thinking the same thing. She would have liked to see where that went. She was more than attracted to him and not just because he was famous and looked like he could have been a cover model for one of the books she sold.

The lingering thought that he could be offering a relationship because of the Media attention and not because he would have wanted more than a night was what stopped her from taking his offer.

There was no hope a man like Joey White was going to call her when this died down and that thought saddened her.

"Amber, you don't have to stay," Baylor said closing her eyes.

"The Nurse will check on you every two hours. Call me if there's a problem. The crowd outside thinned when they spotted Austin and Sydney leaving. You should be good by morning. I can send a car."

"We can catch a cab. Thank you so much," Maren answered for Baylor.

"And then there were two. You don't have to stay Maren."

"I'm the reason you're hurt. I'm staying."

"I am not blaming you, Maren. The concert was great. You got to meet the band."

"You passed up the offer of a lifetime," Maren taunted.

"I thought you weren't going to say it."

"It couldn't be helped. You liked him. I know you. You *really* liked him. You weren't just being nice. Did he kiss you when you were alone?"

"Maren, I didn't kiss him and he didn't kiss me. He only asked me out because the world thinks I'm already his girlfriend."

"I saw the way he looked at you and so did you."

"For all I know, he looks at all women that way. It's over. Our brush with fame is immortalized in pictures, thanks to Amber. You were up-close and personal with your favorite band for hours. Take the win. I need sleep."

"You are right. Go to sleep."

"I'm trying," Baylor smiled as her exhaustion pulled her under.

9

Even in a private room, resting at the hospital isn't possible. Because of her head injury, someone came in every two hours to wake her up.

Baylor's head still hurt. Her vision was better, but the lights in the room were painful, even though she wasn't looking at them directly.

When Finley showed up, Maren, who had stayed the night in a lounge chair, was back to fangirling

Maren had told Baylor the whole story, how she and Griff fell in love and the disaster that happened at Sydney and Austin's wedding. Normally, Baylor wouldn't be that invested in celebrity gossip, but now she actually knew the people in the story.

"Thank you, you didn't have to do this," Baylor said as Finley herself drove both of them to Baylor's place.

"I like to follow through with my patients," Finley smiled.

"Thank you, I'm sure you had something better to do."

"Not really, last night was the end of this tour. I quit my job here at the hospital to travel with the guys. Right now, they are staying here for the next six months."

"They are staying here in town?" Maren squealed.

"No, but in the area."

"Sorry I know that having your privacy is a big deal," Maren said as if she knew what it was like to be famous. Baylor smiled at her friend. She went from rabid fan and back to herself so quickly, it was hard to keep up.

"It is a big deal. We are looking for a place close to family but secluded enough that we can live normally."

"You and Griff. or all of you?" Baylor asked, wondering where Joey lived. Did he have a Penthouse apartment, a house, a mansion? She knew nothing about the man who had swooped in and restored her faith in humanity.

"The guys tend to stick together. I don't think we will share a place, but I have a bet going with the other women that we will be neighbors when they finally decide."

"It's nice that they are still so close." Maren acted like she knew what she was talking about. For all Baylor knew, she probably did.

"It's right up here," Baylor said, squinting despite the fact that Finley had brought her sunglasses, very nice sunglasses.

"That's the bookstore you said you own. I will drop you off at home. You shouldn't be working today." Finley saw the sign up ahead. Baylor's shop was tiny, but she loved it.

"I live above the store. My Manager is handling the store for a day or two."

"Good, I like the name," Finley said about the store's name. "Bookaholic, it's catchy.

"I thought so," Baylor agreed.

"Mind if I look around?"

"Of course not."

Baylor knew that the moment that Finley left, the adventure of the night before would be over. In a day or two, the stitches would be taken out and a viral GIF of her hitting her head over and over with sound effects added would be replaced by some other crazy thing caught on camera.

"Amber asked that I give you her number. I'd also like you to have mine. Call if you have any problems."

"It's a bump on the head and it wasn't the band's fault. Rascal can't be responsible for the actions of the fans. I appreciate all that you have done."

The three ladies walked into the shop and Baylor felt instant relief. The shop was warmly lit with nooks and crannies here and there that people could sit and read. There was little overhead lighting, just a smattering of antique lamps and comfy chairs.

"This is wonderful," Finley gasped, seeing the set up. The rows of books were lined up so you could see the entire store from the front door. "You have a banned book section?" Finley grinned.

"Yes, too many classics are being taken out of the schools or criticized for offensive language. It's not that the content is X-rated like some people think. It's classics that were written in a different time. Everybody is offended by something, so when a School district decided that some book is not suitable to be taught any longer, they can find it here. I have a group of teens that come on Thursday nights to read and discuss banned classics."

"That's a great idea. As a teen, if someone said not to do something, it just made me want to do it more." Finley wandered over, touching the spines and reading the titles.

"I make sure that the more sexually explicit romances are on the other side of the store."

"That's where I like to go," Maren pointed to the Romance section.

"I thought I heard your voice," Barbara, Baylor's Store Manager, came out from the back. "I thought you weren't... Baylor, what happened?" Barbara said, spotting the bandage.

"She was attacked," Maren said before Baylor could answer.

"Attacked... wait, Bay, did you go to a concert last night?" The question seemed odd coming from Barbara. She was a fifty-five-year-old woman with two kids and didn't seem the type to follow the Concert scene.

"Yes, why?"

"It was you. Junie called and said, 'Mom, Baylor is trending'. She sent me the video, but I could not tell if it was you. It was you, wasn't it?"

"I'm going to say yes, since I don't know what you saw exactly."

"I told Junie it had to be a set-up, a stunt. Since when does a performer jump off the stage to help a fan?"

"Since last night," Baylor said as she removed her glasses.

"Oh, wow, that looks terrible," Barbara said, seeing the black eyes that Baylor had awakened to.

"It looks worse than it is. Thanks for coming in so early."

"Not a problem, you go rest. I will call Gretchen if we get busy."

"Did the Edwards' order come in?"

"Yes, I've got this, go."

"Thanks, Barbara."

"Anything for my famous boss. Wait until I tell Junie she was right."

"Please don't? I'm hoping this just blows over. The press doesn't have my name or where I live and work. I'd like to keep it that way."

"Of course, I won't say a word but, Baylor, people are going to see your face and know it was you for sure."

"That is why I will be taking a couple of days off and investing in good cover-up. I've had enough fame for a lifetime."

10

"Finley called. She said the girl is fine," Joey's mother reported as Joey came down to breakfast. Spending the night in his childhood bedroom just motivated him to find a place to live for at least the next six months.

"I doubt she's fine, but it's good to hear," Joey said, searching for his cell phone to text the guys.

"You're looking at houses, I hear. You know that you can always stay with me."

"No offense, Mom, but one night and I already feel like I'm twelve. I need a grown-up room in a house I can well afford."

"I'm glad to hear you and Griff are settling in the area."

"We are all settling here for now, maybe forever if we find the right set-up."

"Set-up?"

"It's Austin's idea. Although, if you ask me, I think he's just looking for built-in babysitters. His thought is one of those Gated communities but smaller, where we all have a home of our own but are nearby. "

"You are all together all the time anyway."

"Yes, plus it would cut down on the cost of security if we are all in the same place."

"Speaking of security?"

"Yasmine is fine. We still are just friends and she's very happy with her current man."

"That's nice, but I was going to ask what happened to the woman that hurt that girl. I heard she bit Rufus."

"That reminds me, I need to go to the station to sign my statement. I don't know what happened with her. I'll see if the police will tell me anything."

"They will. Just find a nice Female officer and ask. No one can turn down a simple request from my Joey."

"Not true, the girl that got hurt shot me down hard."

"How so?" Jane White knew her son's reputation was not good when it came to the ladies.

"I asked her to dinner, coffee, anything, but she said no."

"Did she tell you why? I knew your reputation would come back to haunt you," she scolded.

"I think it was more because the media already assumes we are a couple."

"And she doesn't like that?"

"Not at all, she's... different."

"Different than all of the other girls that would take you up on dinner and more?"

"Yes."

"You never did like to be told no. She sounds like a smart girl."

"Smart because she turned me down? You're my mother, aren't you supposed to be on my side?"

"I am on your side. Can you honestly say that any of your women friends in the past three years have been someone you would settle down with?"

"Oh, so now, you have me settling down with her."

"No, but what little I do know about her is what you need."

"And how much do you know about Baylor?"

"Baylor, I even like her name." So did Joey, but he wanted to hear what his mother had to say. "You were attracted to her?"

"Yes, that's fair."

"She turned you down."

"How is that a plus?"

"It's time you had to work for a real connection, one that isn't in the dark after a show then gone the next day."

"Ouch, I didn't know you thought so poorly of me."

"I think the world of you and your sister. I don't like your track record with women. You have every right to do as you wish, but I think you're missing out. All of the other boys figured that out."

"You think that because all of the others are married or getting married that I should too?"

"No, not until you are ready. I just want to see you happy, Joey."

"I'm pretty happy. I do see what you're getting at. "

"If Griff Johnson can commit, maybe, you should try it. He is crazy in love with your sister and happier than I've ever seen him."

"I will consider your advice. The only woman I've been even slightly interested in in months shot me down last night."

"Was it because she didn't want you, or because she didn't want the public to get the wrong idea?"

"I jumped off stage. The public already has the wrong idea."

“Why did you jump off the stage in the middle of a show? Rufus and his team usually take care of what happens on the floor.”

“I just acted. She’s…”

“Different,” his mother smiled, ending the discussion.

Despite the band’s fame, the town was used to them being home. The locals were kind and gave them their privacy. That didn’t mean walking around town was a good idea. The people just visiting were still in the area after last night’s concert.

“I have a proposition,” Austin said when Joey answered his call.

“I’m sorry, I don’t date married men,” Joey quipped.

“Can you meet us around one o’clock today?”

“Sure, where?”

“I’m texting you the address.”

“That’s all I get, just an address?”

“You will understand when you get there,” Austin explained before hanging up.

Joey had no idea what Austin was up to. In addition to being the Lead Singer, Austin was also the one that had the idea to form a band in the first place. Joey trusted his judgment.

“I’m going out, Mom.”

"Will you be home for dinner?"

"I don't know." Joey loved being home but couldn't help bet feel like a kid when he was. "Austin has us meeting up. I'll let you know."

"Finley said you were all looking for your own place, locally."

"We are."

"Good."

"Are you sick of me already, Mom?" Joey teased.

"No, but you are grown. You should be making your own home. With all of the other boys settling down, it's nice to think they will be close."

"It will be different. With weddings and babies, it's good to know we have a home to go to."

"Maybe, it's time you found someone to come home to?" Joey knew that she was leading the conversation that way all along.

"Yes, maybe it's time?" he called back before leaving to meet the others.

11

Joey reached the address that Austin had given him and all he saw was an iron gate and the driveway beyond.

The gate was open so Joey started up the long driveway. It was actually more of a private road than a driveway and soon a huge home came into view then another. Six homes in all sat on lots that seemed to go back forever. An island of land, a lush garden sat in the middle of the area where the road curved back around, leading back out the way he had come. Austin, Sydney, Griff, and Finley waved him over as they stood with a woman Joey didn't know.

"We are just waiting for Race and Teagan now," Austin said looking pleased with himself.

"Do you mind cluing me in?" Joey scanned the seemingly empty neighborhood.

"This compound is available."

"Compound?" Joey questioned.

"Originally, the man who built this had intended it to be a place where his three sons and two daughters could live next door to one another," the woman who still hadn't introduced herself explained.

"I take it that didn't work? "Griff smiled.

"No, some infighting and jobs taken out of state led the owner to stop construction. He hadn't consulted his children and had planned to surprise them. I have to tell you if someone surprised me with a house like this, I'd be grateful," the Realtor smiled. "I'm Amanda, you must be Joey."

The woman's tone and predatory gaze told Joey that the woman knew exactly who all of them were. In addition to one hell of a commission, she was aiming a different kind of gaze at the only single person there.

"Yes, I'm joey. So, these look nice. You said he ended construction. What's unfinished about them?"

"I'm glad you asked," the woman was in full sales mode now. "The two to our right are unfinished inside. The landscaping in the back was halted as well. It wouldn't take too long to have the work completed."

"Here's Race and Teagan now," Austin cut off the woman's sales pitch.

"I assume your idea is that we live here in this compound?" Joey asked Austin, watching the women go ahead with the realtor.

"It was Sydney's idea."

"I like the idea. I woke up in a twin bed this morning and my mother grilled me about Baylor."

"Baylor, the woman from the concert?"

"Finley called to tell me she was fine."

"I hear she turned you down," Austin laughed.

"Actually, she said no, but that I was free to call her when this blew over. She didn't want to lie and say we were something we are not. Her friend, Maren, who by the way is hilarious, suggested she pretend to be my fake girlfriend."

"Does Maren know you've barely ever had a real girlfriend?"

"You're one to talk. Every one of you were just as bad as I am before meeting the right girl."

"I was joking. Do you actually plan on calling this girl when your heroic stage dive is a distant memory?"

"Yes, I think I will call her. There's something there that caught my eye and, even with the disaster that night was, she was sweet and funny. A lot of girls would have jumped at the chance of being my fake girl just because of who we are."

"Then, in that case, I wish you luck. Let's go see if the girls already bought the place. You don't have to buy in, Joey, not if you don't want to."

"I like the idea, but there are only four of us and six houses."

"I wanted talk to all of you and see if we should offer Amber and Mark a chance to take one. The other we can convert into a studio."

"The neighbors won't be complaining about the noise with this plan."

"Does that mean you're in?"

"I'd like to see the houses first, but yes, I think this is a great idea."

The Realtor, having picked up on the idea that the four might buy all six homes, was flirting less and selling more. That didn't mean that she left Joey's side as they toured the homes.

In the past years, Joey might have enjoyed flirting back with the woman and more. He had no interest in the Realtor at all.

"I heard Mr. Day say something about making one home a studio," the woman gestured to the last home in the semi-circle. "This home has no finished interior. You could build to suit your needs. The vaulted ceilings add to the acoustic advantages of the home."

Joey smiled at the woman then looked to Race, who was having a rough time keeping a straight face. The vaulted ceilings would not be an advantage. It would be the opposite. Joey had to give the woman points for trying, but it was clear she had no idea what she was talking about when it came to building out a Studio space.

"Can you give us a second?" Austin said as the woman hovered.

"Of course, take your time. I will be just outside if you have any questions."

Joey and the others watched her leave before Austin looked at the group.

"So, what do you all think?"

"I love the idea," Teagan smiled at Race, who would follow his fiancé into hell if she asked.

"We are in," Race smiled.

"Fin?" Griff looked at Joey's sister with the same devotion that Teagan had for Race and Sydney had for Austin.

Joey was surprised at his own reaction. He wanted that. He wanted a partner, someone who he could count on to be by his side no matter what.

All three of his friend's had found their person. All three had waded through the fake women and gold diggers that wanted the fame and the money more than the man.

Baylor came to mind. She could have taken him up on his offer. She could have sued the venue or the band, saying the security was lacking. She had even offered to go through her own insurance at the hospital rather than have Rascal's team foot the bill.

He had noticed her not because she was a screaming fan but because she was a genuine fan of the music. He doubted it would have mattered what they looked like or how much money they were making. She had been feeling the music, reacting to the words.

"Joey, did you hear me?" Finley's voice snapped him out of the memory he was in.

"What? No, I didn't hear you. I was just thinking."

"About?" Finley smiled at her brother as if she could read his mind.

"Doesn't matter, what was the question?"

"Are you okay living here with us?"

"It's perfect. Why wouldn't I be okay with it?"

"Because your big sister might live next door. Griff just asked me to live with him." Griff wrapped his arms around Finley and kissed the top of her head. It was something that Joey was now used to. One of his three best friends was going to be his brother-in-law. He knew his sister already had the ring. They just hadn't announced it yet.

"I just spent six months on the road with my sister. I think a whole house away will be fine,

"Then, we are doing this?"

"We are," Joey agreed.

12

"I thought you said you were taking a couple days off," Barbara gave Baylor a stern look as she came from the back room of the bookstore.

"I just came down to see how things were going."

"Since I haven't opened the doors yet, yes, it's been pretty quiet," Barbra joked.

"It's always pretty quiet."

"It was until about noon yesterday, then we had a lot of interest."

"You should have come to get me."

"I didn't come to get you intentionally. Junie wasn't the only one to recognize you. I got the feeling that some of the younger women who came in were looking for your hero, not you or old books."

"Great, you're sure?"

"I'm pretty sure."

"Why would they think Joey would be here in the bookshop?"

"Rumor is you've been dating for a while."

"What rumor, Barbara?"

"I put an alert on my phone. Anytime Joey White or Rascal is mentioned, it alerts me."

"How do you even know how to do that?"

"Junie helped. It's gone off a lot. I had to put it on mute. Baylor, they know your name and that you live above the store."

"So what, this is bound to die down," Baylor said, hoping she was right

"Eventually, it will die down as soon as they realize that he's not here, but I'd guess that that isn't happening before those black eyes fade. You look like you've been a few rounds in the ring and lost."

"If you saw the woman responsible, you wouldn't be surprised."

"Have you heard what they plan to do about her? I hope you are pressing charges."

"I am and, apparently, she bit the Head of Security. Last I heard, she is being evaluated in a Psych ward."

"She bit a person?"

"That's what Amber said. She's the Band's Publicist and the Manager's wife."

"Rascal is sure taking care of you. Yesterday, the Doctor coming back to check on you was a nice surprise. I was worried about you upstairs with no one checking in on you."

"Maren stopped by and Finley came before that. I slept most of the day anyway."

"I was secretly hoping that some of the band might drop by as well."

"Barbara, are you a rascal fan?" Baylor grinned.

"I'm a fan of the music. The boys are too young for me. Even if I stood a chance with men that look that good, my husband isn't a fan of me dating," she chuckled.

"No, I suppose he wouldn't be," Baylor said, heading for the front door. It was time to open, so she pulled the blinds open to flip her Closed sign to Open.

Instead of turning the lock, she stepped back.

"Barbara!" she called, not knowing what to do.

"Are you alright?" Barbara asked, responding to Baylor's tone. "Oh my god, Baylor, maybe call that nice Publicist or maybe we should call the police," Barbara said as soon as she saw what was upsetting Baylor. She was already taking her phone from her pocket.

The crowd outside was now aware that Baylor was on the other side of the door. There had to be at least ten people in view and they were blocking a good amount of the sidewalk and street beyond, so there could have been more.

"They haven't done anything wrong," Baylor looked at her older manager for help.

"Then, open the door. I don't know what to do with this kind of crowd. Three people coming in at the same time is considered a rush."

"I'll call Amber if they get out of hand. When they see that the Band members aren't here, they might just go. Maybe, they don't know who I am."

"Seriously, have you looked in the mirror?"

"Right, I forgot. Here goes. They aren't here to hurt me."

"I wouldn't be so sure. Some women think they have a claim on famous people, even if they haven't met them. Might I remind you that there's a woman in the Psych ward right now that attacked you."

"She was insane and upset that we had free tickets."

"Fine, but I have 911 on speed dial."

"Is he here?" one of the younger patrons squealed as the women pushed into the bookstore.

"No if you're referring to Joey White, he isn't here. He hasn't ever been here and I doubt very much he ever will be," Baylor said to the ten plus women now crowding the store. Her shop was near capacity and none of the women seemed to want to browse, so the aisles were empty.

"How did you and Joey meet?"

"We met when I was pushed into the stage."

"It happened before?" one young woman looked at Baylor with wide-eyes.

"No, it happened only once, two days ago, and before that, I had never met Joey or any of the others. He helped me off the floor and the Band's Medical staff took me to the hospital."

"If you're into fiction, we have an extensive collection of made-up romances down that aisle," Barbara said, trying to be helpful.

"We all saw the way he looked at you," a rather rude woman snapped.

"Believe what you want. I met him once. I met the entire band that night and haven't seen them since. If you'd like something to read, I can show you what we have."

"When he touched you, did you get goosebumps?" a starry-eyed fan asked and Baylor sighed.

"I was trying not to pass out, from the concussion I sustained," she said while walking toward the back room. "If you need help, Barbara will assist you."

"Is Joey hiding back there?" another called and Baylor knew that the women were going to believe what they wanted to. She needed help getting them out of the store, so real customers could shop.

She had two choices. Three if you counted the contact, Joey. He had put his contact information into her phone as a courtesy. He had already come to her rescue once. The crowd in her store was because he had rescued her in the first place. Calling Joey was the opposite of the right thing to do. Calling the police was probably overkill since, so far, the people looking for a famous musician in her tiny bookstore had just been annoying, not dangerous.

"Hello Baylor," Amber answered on the third ring.

"I'm sorry to bother you, but I wasn't sure what to do."

"Is something wrong? Do you need to go back to the hospital?"

"No, I'm healing just fine, according to Finley. I have a crowed at my store looking for Joey. They were actually looking for me, assuming he'd be here. I'm just not sure how to handle that kind of attention."

"I'm on my way."

"You don't have to come. I just didn't know how to get rid of them. You deal with fans all the time."

"And some don't take no for an answer. You need help or you wouldn't have called. I'll call our security to help."

"I don't want to take security away from the people that need it."

"It sounds like you need it."

"I just don't think they believe that I don't really know the band."

"They saw the only single Rascal member carry you off like a bride on her Wedding day. They saw something that, to them, could only mean there's something between you and Joey. Famous musicians don't normally stop the show to help a fan. We have security for that reason. Even I was hoping there was..."

"Why would you hope there was something between us?"

"He needs a good woman and you seem like you'd be perfect for him. His reputation for going through women like a man with a cold goes through tissues is hard to keep up with. What he did, jumping off the stage, was heroic and romantic. My life would be easier if all of them were settled down with girlfriends or wives."

"That's why you thought Maren's fake girlfriend idea was a good idea?"

"No, a fake girlfriend could end up a disaster. If he was seen with another woman but assumed to be with you, the press would have a field day. I was thinking you two should try being in a real relationship. I've looked at the footage of the incident with the police. The way he was watching you before, it's no wonder the fans think there's more to this."

"I know nothing about him or the way he looked at me or any other woman in the front row. All I'm sure of right now is that my bookstore is full of delusional women that think stalking him by crashing a store owned by his supposed girlfriend is a good idea."

"The price of fame, someone will be there soon. Rufus is hard to miss. You'll know when he arrives. I'm about five minutes out."

"Thank you, Amber."

"I have a feeling this isn't the end of the Baylor and Joey story in the press."

"I'm starting to see that," Baylor sighed.

13

Austin made sure that he wasn't pushing the issue. They had all talked about living near one another. Griff had almost talked them into buying an abandoned hotel at one point, years ago. They didn't buy the hotel in the end because Race was sure it was haunted. It wasn't haunted, as far as Joey could tell, but once the idea was out there, buying the place was out of the question.

"Alright, then we're buying all six?" Austin asked for the tenth time.

"Yes, you three can decide which ones you want first. You have wives and babies on the way."

"Race and I don't have wives… yet," he said with a grin while looking at Finley.

"That's just a matter of when, not if. All of the houses are beautiful, far more than I thought I'd ever be able to afford in my lifetime."

"Same here," Griff nodded, "go make the Realtor's day, Austin."

"I think a date with Joey would make her day, from the look of it."

"She's going to have to settle on her commission. I'm not interested."

Joey let Austin do the talking. They were successful enough that buying a row of homes was probably a write-off on their taxes or something, especially if one of the homes was converted into a Studio space.

None of the homes were outrageous. They were large and expensive but not the multimillion-dollar mansions their fans assumed they lived in. Right now, they all lived with relatives temporarily. A house, or even an apartment, had been just a waste of money, since they spent the last three years on the road.

He sat on the patch of well-manicured lawn that created an island as the road curved around it to head back to the main street. He could see the women making this into a play park when they all had kids.

He looked at his sister, who was beaming. Griff made Finley happy. Never in a million years would he have thought Griff would settle down with one woman. The fact that he had chosen Joey's sister had been concerning at first. His friend and his sister were clearly in love. His worry about Griff hurting her or Finley being just another passing phase, which would make holidays awkward, were gone. They had the kind of forever love that Austin and Sydney had. Even Teagan and Race were bound to grow old together.

"This would be a nice spot for a wedding," Joey said aloud.

"Whose wedding are you thinking about?" Race looked at him as if he had two heads.

"Yours, theirs," Joey pointed to his sister and Griff, who were sharing a private moment.

"Not yours?" Teagan grinned.

"Who would I marry, Teagan?"

"He's right. Who would have him?" Race joked.

"I was thinking maybe you could try a little harder with Baylor. It would make my life and Amber's a lot easier."

"How so?"

"If you were really a couple, then it would be out in the open. There would be no speculation, no fans thinking you two are hiding something. The reaction to the footage right before you jumped is swoon worthy."

"Swoon worthy, what the hell is swoon worthy?" Race laughed.

"Comments like 'I wish someone would look at me like that", or 'He's done for'. The way you looked at Baylor in the moments before she was shoved is right out of a Romance novel. You were looking at her with an intensity most woman can practically feel."

"I was looking at her..."

Joey wasn't about to admit that he had felt something click. They had a moment. He was sure of it, one moment where everyone else faded away and she seemed to see him. Joey White, not the bassist, not the musician, not a man with money and fame, just Joey.

"Wow, where did you just go?" Teagan laughed. "Joey, if you really like this girl, why aren't you doing something about it?"

"I am leaving her alone temporarily. When all of the rumors slow down, I will call her. She thinks the only reason I asked her out was because the press already thinks we are together. I want her to know that's not the reason at all."

"You do plan on seeing her then?"

"I plan on asking her to give me a chance. I don't know what her answer will be. I think we connected, but maybe it was just me."

"Ironic, isn't it?" Race mumbled.

"What's ironic, Race?"

"The one girl you show genuine interest in shoots you down."

"It's not like Teagan ran into your arms either."

"True, but she didn't run away." Race was joking. Joey know he was poking fun.

Teagan's cell phone pinged, signifying an incoming text. The scowl on her face right before she glanced his way was not comforting at all.

"Joey, if you're really interested in Baylor, I'm not sure waiting until this dies down is the right thing to do," Teagan handed him the phone so he could read the text.

"I should go," he said, seeing that Amber had sent Rufus to Baylor's bookshop and that she was on her way there herself.

"No, you should stay here, let them handle it, but you should talk to her. Going there will make this ten times worse right now."

"You're right. I'll call her. I have her number."

"She gave you her number? That's a good sign."

"I hope so."

14

Amber was right. Rufus was hard to miss. The nearly seven-foot-tall, dark-skinned giant wearing a Hawaiian shirt and sandals would have stood out, even if he hadn't been with a blonde spirit in a flowing skirt and a tank-top.

"Well, isn't this lovely. Come on in, Honey. Ladies, what's the deal? Are they giving away free tickets here?" the blonde asked.

"She's dating Joey White."

"Oh, I don't think so. Joey White is out house hunting with my niece right now."

"Your niece?"

"On my honor, I'm sure you'll read about it. You do read, don't you?"

"Listen, Lady, I think you are making that up."

"The name is Olivia. I am telling the truth. Joey White is currently house hunting with my niece. Now, if you're not going to buy anything, I'd suggest you leave. My husband doesn't like tight spaces."

The ladies looked at Rufus, who didn't have to say a word to be menacing.

"It says here that Rascal's Band members were spotted house hunting together in the next town over. The Realtor just posted a selfie," one of the younger fans looked intently at her phone.

"If this woman was really his girl, he'd be here, wouldn't he? You can't possibly believe Joey White would leave his girl's side when she's clearly still injured," Olivia glared at the much younger crowd. "Now, I think that you should at least buy something before you all go. Don't you think so, Honey?"

The Giant nodded.

Barbara looked on as if this was the best show in town and all Baylor could think was that Joey was house hunting with this woman's niece, yet he had asked her to dinner less than two days ago.

It didn't take long for the women to disperse, at least for now.

"Rufus, I assume," Baylor said, extending her hand.

"Yes."

"And Olivia, is Joey really house hunting with your niece?" Baylor wanted to kick herself. She had no claim, fake or real on the man.

"Yes, Teagan, Race's fiancé is my niece. Joey is still single as far as I know."

"I didn't mean. I... thank you."

"She loves messing with the fans. I'll post a watch, but the rumor that he's across town should keep them away for now."

"Right until they decide he's cheating on you and start sending you stuff," Olivia laughed

"What stuff? You know what, I don't need to know. Maybe, someone to watch the store for a bit is a good idea."

Baylor's cell phone started to ring and she sighed. If the fans got her number, she'd have to change it.

The caller ID said Joey White.

"Hello."

"Baylor, are you alright? Did Rufus get there?"

"Yes, Rufus is here and he brought his secret weapon," Baylor answered.

"Olivia is there," he said to someone else. "I almost made it worse. I'm sorry."

"Made it worse, how?"

"I was ready to rush over there."

"Oh, um, you're really nice to want to save me again. They were annoying and insisted I was dating you, even though I told the truth."

"Then, date me."

"I'm a mess right now, Joey. I'm sure you can find another girl that doesn't need saving all the time."

"The way I remember it, you needed saving both times because of me. I looked at you like you hung the moon. Those are Sydney's words, although hanging the moon would be impressive."

"I will think about it. I'm still functioning on maybe 60 percent. I can't read or watch TV without it making my head pound. I'm not making any decisions right now."

"Hold on, Finley… she's having trouble..." Joey's voice faded for a second then came back. "She says that is pretty normal. Are you throwing up anymore?"

"That's right. I puked on you "

"You missed. Race had a bucket handy.

"I'll think about it," Baylor couldn't help but smile.

"Can I call you?"

"Yes."

"That's a good start. Is there someone there to help right now?"

"Barbara, my Manager, has it well in hand. Unless another ten or more fans show up, then Rufus is sending someone to handle it."

"Good to hear. Get some rest."

"I will. Thanks for calling." Baylor hung up, smiling at her phone. When she looked up, Barbara, Olivia, and Rufus were all staring.

Amber's arrival was a saving grace. Baylor didn't want to have the discussion about just going ahead and dating the man with Barbara or these two virtual strangers.

"Those eyes need some ice," Olivia commanded.

Barbara pointed to the back room and the staff fridge as Amber thanked Rufus for coming on his day off.

"Baylor, I should have anticipated this. I'm so sorry. I didn't think they had identified you yet."

"It was fine, until they started insisting that she was lying. I don't want to go to jail, but if someone else comes in here and calls Bay a liar, I might punch the bitch," Barbara barked

Baylor burst out laughing, which hurt like hell and made her hold her face to stop the pain.

"Bay, I'm so sorry."

"Don't be. That's the funniest thing I ever heard you say."

"I mean it."

"No one is going to jail," Rufus smiled as Olivia came out with ice. His smile made him look only slightly less dangerous. "You will have someone here by this evening to intervene if needed."

"The store closes at five today."

"But you live above it, am I correct?"

"Yes."

"Someone will be watching."

"That's not creepy at all. How am I supposed to tell the Security team from the stalkers?"

"You won't even notice the stalkers because we will see them first," he said with confidence.

15

"I heard you were buying a house." Baylor had spoken to Joey at least once a day for the rest of the week. It was now exactly one week since he had jumped off the stage and carried her off the Arena floor.

"We are all buying a neighborhood. It's six houses in a gated community. I'd tell you the address, but then I'd have to kill you."

"That secret, huh?"

"No, not really, we will have security at the gate."

"Your security is really good. I haven't had any mobs at the store since that for first day. A few curious teens mostly have come in to see if I have you hidden in my closet."

"I should show up one day and see their reaction."

"I think that would just start the rumors up again."

"The rumors that we are dating?" Joey asked.

"Yes, and all the others, Barbara's daughter has made a list. I am not only dating you. You're cheating on me with that Realtor you were pictured with."

"She took a selfie when I wasn't looking."

"I wasn't accusing you of cheating, Joey. You can't cheat if we aren't really dating. I'm apparently also carrying your child. Finley stopping by to remove the stitches on Tuesday was a clear sign that she is on my side of the argument."

"You'll learn not to read the things people say online."

"I know the truth, so I'm just enjoying the absurdity of it all."

"It's not absurd. I still want that date you promised."

"I don't recall promising a date."

"You said when you could think straight, you'd go out with me. Dinner, lunch, I'll take what I can get."

"Why?" Baylor asked out loud, wishing she hadn't.

"Why would I want a date? Baylor, I'm sure that you and I were meant to meet. I can't get you out of my head."

"Have you been trying to get me out of your head?"

"Not really, I've been trying to talk my self out of just driving over and knocking on your door. I am ridiculously attracted to you. I was the moment I spotted you in the front row. I want to date you not because they already think we are a thing, but because I think we should be a thing. We talk daily. I look forward to talking to you. "

"I look forward to it as well."

"So, let me take you to dinner. I can find a place that we won't be noticed."

'Where, the moon?"

"No, we have private places that protect our privacy."

"I'm not sure I'm ready for the level of attention you and I actually dating would get."

"I think I'm worth it. I can't help who I am or that people will care who I'm seeing and make stuff up that may be true or might be pure fantasy. I haven't been this interested in a woman ever. I have never had to put this much work into getting a date, ever."

"Is that supposed to impress me?" Baylor asked.

"No, it's supposed to show you that you are special. We are perfect together. I think you might even see that yourself. I'm part of a band that's well known. I have fans. I have a public life as well as a private life. It's the cost of fame. I will understand if that's a deal breaker, but I hope it isn't."

"It's not a deal breaker, Joey. it's a 'Proceed with Caution' sign. The woman that pushed me didn't shove me because Maren and I were making noise. She apparently shoved me because you looked at me with that smolder."

"Smolder?"

"You really don't read the stuff they put online, do you?"

"Amber and Teagan filter the stuff I need to know. How do you know she shoved you because of me?"

"It's in the report I got from the police. She told the person evaluating her that I was a threat to her, not the other way around."

"And what she said to her doctor was not confidential. I thought there were rules."

"Apparently, her admission was considered an on-going threat to me, so the therapist, or whoever, had to inform the police."

"She's still in the hospital?"

"For now, they are going to try and determine if she's sane enough to stand trial. She assaulted me in front of hundreds of cameras and the video of the concert. I doubt I'd even have to testify. "

"And she bit Rufus."

"I met Rufus earlier this week. He's terrifying. I can't imagine having the guts to bite him."

"She's clearly insane. Back to dinner or lunch, I will respect your wishes if you want me to back off, but the rumors aren't going to die anytime soon, especially if that woman does end up in a court room. Either way, us having a date or a relationship would just start the rumors up again. Is your head clear enough to decide if you should take the chance?"

"My head is clear."

"What does your gut say? You said you knew that coming to the concert was going to end badly and it did. Maren said if you told me not to get on a plane, I should listen. So, what's your intuition telling you now, Baylor?"

"I feel like pushing you away would be a mistake," Baylor admitted.

"Is that a yes to dinner?"

"Joey, if one date is going to turn my life upside down even more than it is, I would want more. I'm not a one and done kind of girl."

"One and done, that rumor I have heard. I will admit I tend to move on quickly. I generally make sure that the woman isn't expecting more. You are different. I want more than one date. I think maybe our date could be my last first date ever."

"Now that's a line I've never heard before."

"I just feel like, despite your feeling that you shouldn't have gone out last Saturday night, you went out for a reason. I'm not usually one to believe in fate or destiny, but I saw you in the front row and couldn't take my eyes off of you, despite the revealing outfit your friend had on."

"Are you free tomorrow night?"

"Yes, if I wasn't, I am now."

"Then yes, Joey, I'd love to go to dinner with you."

16

"Oh my god, you're going on a date with Joey White." Maren was bouncing on her toes with excitement.

"I'm sure you saw that coming. Just help me hide the left-over bruising."

"You are stunning even with two black eyes."

"They are more green than black now."

"It's not like he wasn't there when you got hurt. Do you know where he is taking you?"

"I don't know."

"Yet, you are trusting him to pick you up. Baylor, you never let a date pick you up the first few times."

"I don't let men I don't really know yet pick me up. I think Joey has proven he's not going to hurt me. I have spoken to him seven days in a row and he has been nothing but a gentleman."

"Baylor, you need a sexy Rock god naked in your bed, not a gentleman."

"Maren, behave."

"I am, but you can't say you haven't thought of the possibilities."

"I like to get to know a person before getting naked."

"Get to know them like talk to them every day after they rescued you from Helga?"

"Her name is actually Sue."

"Well, Sue can rot in the Psych ward, for all I care. "

"I worry about other women's reactions when they find out we are really dating."

"So, this is more than just a date, you are dating?" Maren asked.

"He said that he thought it might be his last first date."

"I'd say that was romantic and all, but Joey didn't really date women. He more hooked-up with them."

"All week, you've been pushing me to go out with him and now your being cynical."

"I was stating a fact. Joey White saying you're his last first date is a big deal. He is really into you, Baylor."

"I got that memo. I'm just hoping he will still be into me, now that has won."

"Men that are as popular and famous don't have to win a woman. The fact that he even tried means that maybe you and he are the real deal. Being your best friend, I will be expecting backstage passes for life."

"You're getting ahead of yourself."

"Am I?"

"Just hand me the cover-up."

For a brief moment, seeing Joey's name on her Caller ID as a call came in, Baylor thought he might be backing out.

"Hello?"

"Baylor, I'm at the back door."

"Oh, I'll be right down," she sighed, grabbing her bag and running down the back stairs. If Maren had still been there, she wouldn't have ever lived down the fact that she nearly tripped racing for the door like a teen.

She opened the door and, without a word, Joey took two steps toward her, placing his hands on either side of her head, cradling her face, then he kissed her lightly on the mouth.

The gesture was both sensual and caring. Her butterflies had butterflies as he pulled back to look at her face.

"I am so glad you said yes."

"I'm pretty glad right now too," Baylor smiled.

"Did I hurt you?"

"By kissing me? No, Joey, I hit my head not my lips."

"In that case..."

Joey leaned in and kissed her again. This time, he took his time. Baylor instinctively stepped into him as he tangled his fingers in her hair, tilting her head up to meet him.

"Woah, no wonder half the girls in town are looking for you," Baylor panted, trying to catch her breath.

"Only half?" Joey smirked.

"You must be slipping."

"I only want you, Baylor."

"We haven't even had our first date. You could change your mind."

"I don't think so. Are you ready?"

"Where are we going?" Baylor said as she locked her door and Joey led her to a non-descript, four door that had seen better days.

"Dinner, then we can go from there."

"I'm not a sure thing, Joey."

"I didn't mean it that way. I thought you might like to see the house I bought."

"Oh, yes, I would."

"Dinner first."

"Is this your car?" Baylor asked, seeing the well-worn seats.

"I bought it with the money from our first few paying gigs. She's not pretty, but she runs well and no one is looking for Joey White in this car."

"I got a small test of what it must be like. All of those people wanting your attention has to be annoying."

"It's flattering. Most are polite and Rufus keeps the crazies at bay. If I had seen the attack on you coming a second sooner, I would have done something."

"Can I ask you something about that?"

"Ask me anything," Joey reached over the center console and took Baylor's hand. It seemed so natural.

"You said you were watching me, that you noticed me specifically."

"I noticed your friend first, then you, to be honest."

"She was practically naked from the waist up. I can't say as I'm surprised."

"I noticed you because you were different. All of the women and some of the men around you were screaming so loudly, I'm surprised they could hear the music. You heard the music. Your eyes were closed. You were swaying in-sync with the rhythm and I could tell you felt it. For someone that said she didn't want to go to see us, you were radiant."

"I never said I didn't want to go. I just had a feeling I shouldn't go."

"I'm glad you did."

"I'm glad I did too, despite the obvious reason my Spidey senses were tingling."

"Spidey senses?"

"It's hard to describe. It was just a feeling, a warning. I can't explain it."

"I go with my gut on some things, like the decision to buy a house this week."

"You said we bought a house, who is we?"

"The guys, maybe Mark and Amber, we bought an entire neighborhood. It's easier to keep secure and we can practice without having to travel."

"Its nice that you're all that close."

"We are and always have been brothers. Griff is going to technically be my brother once he gets his ass in gear and proposes."

"You think he will?"

"I know he is planning to. We are here. I will warn you that I can't guarantee someone won't spot us and out the fact that we are on a date. This place has rules, but people can't help themselves."

"Rules, what rules?"

"This is Randall's. Sydney and her Dad, Hank, own it. It's the first place Rascal ever played."

"I saw the article that was in the paper when they got engaged, epic love story."

"Anyway, the place is always packed. The band has a table of our own in a corner. The rules are if you're eating or drinking at Randall's and someone famous (AKA us) walks in, you need to be polite and respectful."

"Does that work?"

"To an extent, people still take pictures and occasionally ask for an autograph. It's not as bad as most places. Are you ready to go public?"

"That we are on a date?"

"Whatever you're comfortable with. They will assume we are a couple."

"They already do."

"Is that a problem?"

"No, I'm okay with it if you are. Maren said you don't date."

"I tried it once. I'll tell you the story over dinner."

17

Joey was sure that this date was the first of many. He had been serious when he told her it might be his last first date ever. Just kissing her was so much more than he had ever experienced and he had kissed a lot of women.

"Order whatever, you're not one of those women who orders a salad and a water, then goes home and scarfs an entire large pizza, are you?"

"No, and I'm starving. If I'm going on a date with a famous Rock star, I'm getting the steak."

"What, no lobster?"

"Maybe that too," Baylor joked as they walked through the kitchen and out onto the floor. "You weren't kidding about it being crowded."

"It's always like this on the weekends. This way, the table is a little more secluded."

"Do you have a Security team that follows you?"

"That depends on where I'm going. Roy, at the front door, is one hell of a bouncer, in case someone followed us here from your place."

"I keep looking out the window of my place to see if I can spot Rufus and his team."

"The whole point is that they aren't seen. Tell me about you, Baylor."

"What do you want to know?"

"Everything."

"You have to agree to tell me about you then."

"You can google my name. Are you saying you haven't?"

"Oh, I have, but this week has taught me not to trust everything I read. According to many people out there, I've been dating you in secret for a while. The attack was a set-up. I wasn't really hurt and I'm after your money because I own a failing bookstore."

"Is it failing?"

"No, I own the building outright. The taxes aren't too bad. All I need is food and a few other necessities and the Antique Book market is more lucrative than you'd expect."

"Why books?"

"Because my Aunt who lived with us for a while had a love of books. She bought the building, renovated it, and opened the shop. My Mother and Father would leave me there when they had to work. I read almost every book she had one summer."

"Are your parents alive?"

"Yes, they moved to Florida to spend their twilight years. My Aunt passed with no children, so she left the shop and apartment to me. I could have sold it, but I wanted to honor her legacy. Plus, I love it. I make my own hours. I have one full-time and one part-time employee that I can count on and most of my sales are online, so I'm not all that busy during the hours it's open."

"What did teen Baylor want to be when she grew up?"

"An astronaut."

"Really?"

"Yes, but I didn't have the math scores. There is a lot of math."

"I'll bet there is. Favorite color?" Joey leaned back with a wicked smile that was unfair to any woman in his path.

Dinner was delicious. Joey's twenty plus questions got more and more personal and Baylor answered every one. She felt like she had known this man for far longer than a week. She was more and more attracted with every passing minute. She had told him she wasn't a sure thing. Truthfully, she was. Maren was right. She had to seize the moment, take it one day at a time. He didn't date, he didn't have relationships, but this sure as hell felt like they were starting a relationship."

"Scoot over here," Joey patted the space next to him, taking out his phone.

"What are we doing?" Baylor asked with a smile as she slid toward him on the bench seat.

"We are taking a selfie commemorating our first date."

"You sound like you expect there to be more," she was fishing but couldn't help it.

"So many more, is it okay if I post this?"

"Can I see how bad I look?" Baylor leaned into him to see the picture. Her eyes looked black, even with the cover-up. She looked more tired than battered, but it was the best she'd looked since."

"Sure, why not, the worst of it is a Gif with you carrying me off and blood streaming down my face. This is an improvement."

"I'm posting it as a first date."

"That will keep them talking."

"I don't have to post it."

"Go ahead, at least it's the truth."

"I'm glad you said that because there's a guy near the kitchen door that's been taking pictures all night."

"The price of fame, yours I mean. I'm just along for the ride. You promised to tell me why you don't date?"

"I did, didn't I?"

"So, enough about me, tell me why Maren was so surprised you asked me on a date and hinted at more?"

"Oh, there will be more, I hope."

"The date's not over. I can't commit to a second date before we are done with the first. Quit stalling."

"I could say that I didn't date because we were always traveling, but that's not really the truth. I didn't used to date because I am a loyal boyfriend."

"How can you be a loyal boyfriend if you don't date?" Baylor smiled.

"Baylor, there are a lot of temptations out on the road."

"I'll bet."

"I was young and famous and women were throwing themselves at all of us. I chose not to date seriously, so I didn't have to worry that I was being unfaithful to anyone. The women I took on dates knew that there was probably not going to be a second."

"I'm sure many were hoping for a second date though."

"Sure, I guess occasionally there's a woman that doesn't understand the word no. Sydney found a naked woman in the bed she and Austin were sharing at Mark and Amber's wedding. They had been a couple for less than forty-eight hours."

"What did she do?"

"She told the woman to get dressed and get out."

"Since they are married and expecting, I'm going to guess that worked out."

"It worked out because Sydney knew Austin would never commit to her then go back to the way we were in the beginning."

"You said you tried dating once."

"I did. My one and only attempt at long term was a bust. She's one of Rufus's guards, Sydney's personal guards. I knew she had a thing for me and she is a great girl, smart and funny. Finley suggested I try to see if there was more there."

"There wasn't?"

"Not for a lack of trying, we were attracted to one another but that was it, no real spark, no common interest. She knew far more than any woman should about my history with women. We decided to just be friends. She's dating one of the roadies."

"That was very mature of you. Your first real girlfriend still talking to you is a win."

"Yes, and good practice."

"Joey, don't be crass," Baylor scolded jokingly.

"I didn't mean that kind of practice. What I mean is you're different. We have been here for hours and I want to talk to you even more. You eat like a normal person and you're funny. That spark I was missing with Yasmine is very much there between us and all we have done is kiss."

"I liked that kiss very much."

"And on that note, Waitress, check please?"

18

"Where are we going now?" Baylor sat back in her seat. Joey's car ran better than you would think, since it looked like a madman assembled it from parts, they found in the junk yard.

"We are going to look at my new house. Unless, you want me to take you home?"

"I want to see your new house."

"You have to swear never to divulge the secret location."

"You're serous?"

"Not really, but try not to post it."

"I would never."

"I know that's part of your appeal. You are real. You don't care who I am. I feel like you're with me on a date because you wanted to go on a date with me, not the bassist from Rascal."

"Does that happen, people don't see you, just your job?"

"My job or my money, some are looking to further their own career by association."

"No wonder you don't date."

"I didn't date until I met you."

"You really do see us being more, don't you?"

"I told you that before you said yes."

"I've been fed lines before, Joey."

"What are my chances of a second date?"

"Your chances are excellent."

"And a third?"

"We will see."

"I'll take that as a yes."

Joey pulled the car into a long driveway with a Guard hut blocking the road. It looked like they were crossing some European border as a guard stepped out and Joey waved."

"Hey Matt."

"Mr. White, hold on, I'll let you through."

"Thanks, I'm just showing my girl the new house."

"Baylor, right?" the guard ducked his head, looking in the window.

"Yes."

"I saw what happened last week. I wish I could have gotten to you in time."

"Joey managed just fine."

"I'm glad to see you're feeling better. Go on through." The guard opened the gates remotely.

"Your girl?" Baylor asked, giving Joey the side-eye as they passed.

"Yes, I'm manifesting what I want and you are what I want. I mean it, Baylor. This isn't some line. When I saw you that night, I was already plotting a way to convince you to take a chance on a Rock star with questionable dating experience."

"Questionable is an understatement."

"Please tell me you didn't google me?"

"Of course, I did, but I'm here, aren't I?"

"Yes, you are. In the last couple of years, the novelty of being chased has worn off. The others falling one by one made me sort of envious. I want a partner, not arm candy. I want reality. The fantasy aspect of our lifestyle has worn off. I'd like a family one day."

"Kids?"

"Yes, a couple or more, Austin and Sydney have already talked about getting another bus so when we have families, we can take them with us."

"The baby is going on tour."

"Yes, not to the concert because of the sound level, but with us. Other groups have done it."

"So, what does being your girl entail, exactly?"

"Me, for one," Joey said as a few homes came into view. It wasn't quite dark yet and these houses were hard to miss.

"I will put that in the Pro's column."

"The attention."

"Con."

"My luxurious home, there is a pool in back."

"Pro, not that I'm moving in."

"Not yet."

"Go on."

"Free tickets."

"Pro, mostly to keep Maren happy. I might be a little gun shy."

"As my girlfriend, you would be backstage."

"Pro," Baylor smiled.

"Believe it or not, you'd get less attention if we went public."

"How do you figure?"

"The frenzy with the fans is more wondering if we are a couple or not. Was the fan that pushed you a case of jealousy? Were you just in the wrong place at the wrong time? If we give them straight answers, they get bored."

"It's still a Con."

"That's fair. Come, I will show you my new house. There isn't any furniture inside yet. How are you at decorating?"

"Isn't it a little too soon to have me decorating your place? I haven't agreed to being your girl yet."

"Yet, even if you reject me, breaking my heart, I need some advice on furniture. It's a huge, very expensive house and if I'm left to my own devices, it will look like a giant Frat house."

"There are decorators out there who will furnish the entire place for the right price."

"I want to make it comfortable and a home, not some showroom."

"I'll let you know what I think when I see the inside." Baylor took Joey's offered hand, liking the feel of his touch. She liked it a lot and wanted more.

"Will you make out with me by the pool?"

"Why the pool?"

"I have Patio furniture."

"You bought furniture for the outside but not the inside?"

"It's summer and there's a pool."

"You are such a child," Baylor chuckled.

"But you like that?"

"I do, I really do. You are not at all what I imagined."

"Is that good?"

"It's the only reason I'm considering being your girl. There will be rules, Joey."

"Like no making out with anyone else by the pool?" he giggled.

"No making out with anyone anywhere. I know you are staying put for the next few months, but I'd like to make sure you aren't going back to your old ways if we are still a thing when you go back on tour."

"No other women, I won't even talk to any women."

"Don't be ridiculous. They will still throw themselves at you and rub up against you like a cat. That Nurse at the hospital, she couldn't help it. I just want to be assured you're not rubbing back."

19

"We need a bed. Why don't you have a bed?" Baylor said, breaking all of her first date rules. She was more than hot and bothered. She was on fire.

"You have a bed at your place." Joey jumped up from the chair they had been sharing for the last hour or more.

"Yes, I have a bed. I also have a guard that will know you're in my bed."

"Baylor, the guards here know what we were about to do. The whole neighborhood is Security monitored. The upstairs bedrooms are the only thing not wired."

"You know what, I don't think I care. Take me home," Baylor said abruptly.

"Bay, are you upset?"

"No, not at all, I just don't want to ruin the mood."

"I think we could work back up to where we are pretty quickly."

"Too much talk, just drive," Baylor teased as Joey shut down the few lights they had on and rushed out to his car with her.

"I'm ordering a bed tomorrow."

"Good call," Baylor laughed.

By the time they reached Baylor's back door, they were stumbling in, not willing to break the kiss he had started as soon as he helped her out of the car.

"Upstairs," Baylor said, leaving their shoes and his shirt in the wake.

Tearing off each other's clothes, they reached her bedroom and she shoved the ten outfits she had decided not to wear onto the floor.

"Wait, condom," Baylor gasped in a moment of clarity.

"I'm way ahead of you."

"You had those on you the whole time?" Baylor asked looking at the long strip of condoms.

"Force of habit, I always have my own so no one tampers with them."

"Women do that?"

"Do you have any idea how much money we all have?"

"No, and I don't care."

"That's why you're my last first date. Yes, women will poke holes and claim the baby is one of ours."

"Has that happened?"

"Once to Austin."

"Alright, I feel better about the fact that you have enough condoms for a month."

"Oh, Baylor, you have no idea," Joey said, taking her down with him as he flopped onto the bed.

Baylor knew from their first kiss that dating Joey was going to be dangerous to her heart.

He said all the right things and the man knew how to please a woman in bed. That was becoming increasingly evident.

Deciding to take this chance was either the best decision she had ever made or the worst. she couldn't think about the future. His saying this was his last first date could be something he said to many women. She didn't think that was the case. Even his Sister and the other people she had met since his public rescue had indicated he was serious about wanting a relationship.

Her mind was reeling, her body was on fire, and this man was worth the risk. If he walked away after this, she'd feel foolish, but this would still be one hell of a memory.

"Baylor, look at me," Joey said as she was about to lose her mind.

Sex for Baylor had always been beautiful and natural. It was an emotional act, a connection between two people. This seemed different. This seemed like more. Joey White was making love to her. Gazing into his eyes as they reached their peak at the same time, she saw what the media did. This moment was theirs. No one else existed. He was seeing her and she was seeing him in a way that was personal and private.

Twice more, Joey woke Baylor and made it clear to her that this was more for him as well. In the wee hours of the morning, they fell asleep. Joey was curled around her, his arm draped across her. The weight of him was reassuring. Famous Rock gods probably never spent the night. At least, that's what she told herself.

Breaking her own rules for Joey White was not something she would regret. She was taking the fact that he stayed as a good sign.

When Baylor woke in the late morning, Joey was sitting on the edge of her bed looking out the small window.

"Joey?" she asked hesitantly. There was nothing to look at outside the window, since it faced a brick wall, yet he hadn't moved.

"Baylor, I don't know how to do this."

"This? What *this* are we talking about, the this where you break it to me that you're leaving and tell me what a nice time you had then never call, or this about us together all night in my bed?"

"Neither, I'm not planning on ghosting you ever. I do have to leave eventually, but I plan to come back. I just don't know how to do this relationship thing. Do I go? Do I stay? Do I take you out to breakfast? Is it too early to propose?"

"Yes, it's too early to propose," Baylor laughed, feeling much better. "Breakfast might be a bad idea since you will be wearing the same clothing from last night. What do you want to do?"

"I want to go online, order a bed for my place, then take you back to your bed. Do you have to work today?"

"We open at Noon and Barbara is coming in. I think she could handle things. Why?"

"Will you go shopping with me?"

"For beds?"

"Yes, and a couch, all of the things that make a house a home. I want your input."

"Alright. I'll spend your money on stuff for your house, but I don't know what you like."

"Neither do I. I'd say comfortable is a priority."

"Let me call Barbara and make sure she's okay here alone."

"She's not alone. Rufus has a team outside. "

"Oh, that's right. We were spotted last night at dinner. They will know we are really a thing."

"A thing? We are way more than a thing. You are my girl. We are dating. In case you hadn't noticed, I just proposed," Joey smiled. "I don't care if the world knows."

"And we are actually talking about the world since you are you, aren't we?" Baylor said softly.

"I think I'm worth it," Joey joked.

"I think you are worth it too, or you wouldn't have made it past the first floor. I'll get used to being famous by association."

20

"Baylor, Girl, I need all the details. You are all over the internet," Maren's voice flowed up the stairs.

"Did we not lock the door?" Joey asked, pulling his pants on as Baylor scrambled, throwing on whatever she could grab.

"She has a key," Baylor said, feeling panicked until she looked at Joey's smile.

"Calm down. We are decent," Joey said, hugging her to assure her.

"Baylor, is this Joey White's shirt on your landing?" Maren screamed.

"Yes, Maren, it is. We will be out in a minute."

"We… Joey White is in there with you?"

"Why do you always call him Joey White?" Baylor asked, going out to greet her friend.

"Because he's Joey White, not just any Joey. He's here? He's in your bedroom right now, shirtless?"

"Yes, Maren. You need to calm yourself. I can't have my best friend lose her shirt every time he's here."

"Every time? So, there will be more times? Bay, did you sleep with Joey White? You don't do that."

"I apparently do, because I did."

"And she's planning to do it again, I hope," Joey came out, taking his shirt from Maren, who was hesitant to give it up.

"Wow, so, you are…"

"She has agreed to be my girlfriend, Maren. I hope you approve."

"Approve? I've been trying to come up with the perfect couple's name, you know like, Bennifer."

"What have you come up with?" Joey's smirk told Baylor he was enjoying Maren's over the top reaction.

"Well, Jaylor is out and Bayjo was dumb. Boey is sort of taken, even if it's spelled different."

"She really has thought of this," Joey laughed, looking at Baylor.

"Yes, from the moment you jumped off the stage mid-show."

"Maren, maybe we don't need a couple's name. How about we just say Baylor and Joey? Were you saying something about the media?"

"Not just the media, I think you two might blow up the internet once they find out you're really a couple. You are really a couple, aren't you?"

"Yes, Maren," Baylor answered, "now, show me what they are saying on the internet."

"The public can be cruel, Baylor," Joey warned.

"I almost expect it. What does it say, that I was a pity date, that my black eyes were showing?"

"Nothing like that," Maren laughed, "it's mostly about you two being seen having dinner and it seemed intimate."

"I told you once we go public, it will die down. They want a mystery, something sensational. Us dating is neither."

"I would not say that, Joey. People are weighing in on how long you two will last. Some even think it's a publicity stunt."

"This is why I don't read the tabloids," Joey sighed, shaking his head. "They rarely get things right and when they do, it's twisted."

"I better get used to it," Baylor smiled at Joey, assuring him she was on board with this life.

"I will make sure to fact-check everything I read," Maren offered.

"Maybe, you shouldn't read it at all." Baylor scolded.

"Now that I have the inside scoop, I have the real story."

"Here is today's story. We are going shopping for furniture for Joey's new house."

"You've been there?" Maren squealed.

"There she goes again," Joey laughed at Maren's response.

"Yes, and it's just a regular house, big but not a mansion."

"I heard you all have houses in the same neighborhood," Maren looked to Joey.

"We do. That much is true. I can't tell you where it is."

"I don't want to know. I'm terrible at keeping a secret."

"Baylor and I aren't secret. I plan on convincing her I'm the guy for her. I'd appreciate you trying to refrain from mentioning that I spent the night for her sake."

"That's no one's business," Maren grinned.

"Good, now I'm starving. Can I take you two to breakfast?"

"Me... you want me to come?"

"From what I understand, you are the reason Baylor came to the concert last week."

"Yes, and she got hurt."

"I also got him, so I think I do owe you for taking me," Baylor chuckled.

"Oh my god, my best friend is dating Joey White."

"Get it all out before breakfast, Maren. You have to act normal," Baylor scolded, gathering her purse and keys.

"I'll be cool, no sweat, breakfast with Joey White. It happens all the time," Maren muttered to herself as they went down the stairs to Joey's car.

"This hunk of junk is yours?" Maren looked confused.

"You were expecting a limo?" Joey laughed.

"I don't know what I expected. This is so… normal."

"I am normal, Maren."

"Famous people are not normal, but I'll play along."

"Use your Acting skills, Maren."

"Right, I go out to breakfast all the time with famous people," Maren laughed while getting into the back seat.

21

"I like your friend," Joey said after dropping Maren off at her house.

"She's good people. I'm sure her fangirling will die down eventually."

"That sounds like you're planning on sticking with me for a while."

"Last first date, I'm starting to believe you."

"Good, because we have a stop to make before we go shopping."

"I'm not following."

"You will see. We are here."

Baylor saw the modest home in a regular neighborhood they had pulled up in front of. Joey was already out of the car and had her door open before Baylor could ask whose home it was.

The answer was clear when an older woman who looked just like her daughter came out to greet them.

"You are taking me to meet your mother?" Baylor hissed, suddenly nervous.

"I need to change clothes and yes, I want you to meet my mother."

"Well, this is a first," the woman smiled. "Baylor, I assume." It made Baylor feel good that the woman knew her name.

"Yes, it's a pleasure to meet you Mrs. White."

"Call me Jane."

"Alright, Jane."

"Mom, I'm going to go change and grab a few things," Joey called.

"We will be fine. If she can survive the attention you get, when in public, I'm sure she can survive me."

"She's harmless," Joey smiled, then he kissed her quickly.

Baylor knew she was probably beet red as she was ushered inside.

"How is your head feeling? I heard what happened."

"It's much better than it was a week ago."

"I was surprised to hear my boy jumped off the stage, but I can see why now. You are stunning, Baylor."

"Black eyes and all, thank you."

"You should also know that you are the first woman Joey has brought home."

"He is here to change."

"And pick up a few things. He didn't come in last night. I know there's no furniture in that house of his."

"We are going shopping today to get him at least something to sit on."

"Oh, have you seen the house?"

"Yes, he showed me the house last night."

"I'm going to stick my nose in just this once. Joey doesn't bring women home. He wouldn't have shown you his home and asked you to help furnish it unless you mattered to him. He's a good man, my Joey is. I hope you plan on giving him a chance."

"I do plan on seeing where this goes, Jane."

"Good, that's what I wanted to hear. Can I interest you in a cookie or a drink?"

"I'm fine. We just had breakfast."

"You be sure to let me know if he's not taking care of you."

"Your family has already gone above and beyond for me."

"As it should have."

"Mom, I hope that you are being nice to my girl?" Joey said intentionally.

"I was about to break out the Baby pictures. There's the cutest one of you in the tub…"

"Mom!"

"I am joking. He was a funny looking kid. Go buy furniture. I won't expect you tonight either. I look forward to seeing you again, Baylor."

"I do too, Jane," Baylor smiled as Joey dragged her out the door.

"I probably should have warned you."

"Your Mom is great. Is it true that I am the first girl you ever brought home?"

"Not really, we brought Sydney into our lives as sort of a mascot early on when Austin was too chicken to tell her what he felt."

"He knew that early?"

"Half of our songs are about Sydney. She had no idea."

"Maren said something about that. I will admit I didn't listen. I love your music, but I didn't really care about your personal lives."

"They get it wrong a lot. If you do decide you want to know something, ask us."

"I will. So, I'm the second woman you brought home to meet your mother?"

"Yes, I thought I'd better do it right away before she gets ahold of the tabloid."

"You just said the tabloids are mostly wrong."

"Mostly, but based on truth. For all I know, the Breakfast date is in the news as a threesome, a break-up, or a Wedding Planning secession, since Maren is your best friend."

"It's been a week and they already have us getting married."

"Remember, they think it's been longer and, with Syd and Austin getting married and Teagan and Race getting engaged, they assume correctly that Griff will get married to Finley, so my having a girlfriend and planning to follow their lead makes perfect sense to them. They build this fantasy then tear it down."

"If I was Teagan, I'd suggest running away to Las Vegas."

"Has it been a lifelong dream of yours to be married by Elvis? These are things I need to know," Joey smirked.

"No, I haven't thought about a wedding much at all since I had no one I wanted to marry."

"Don't all little girls dream of their wedding?"

"This little girl saw through the Fairy tales. When I was ten, I wrote an alternate ending to Cinderella. It took place after the wedding to the Prince."

"The happy ending?"

"A more realistic one where Cindy, that's what I called her, finds that the Prince is shallow. He was just grabbing the first pretty girl to shut his parents up about taking a wife and he had a foot fetish."

"You didn't..." Joey laughed. "How would a ten-year-old even know what a foot fetish was?"

"I didn't know what it was exactly. I had just heard the term. It's not fit to print if you know the real definition."

"Please, tell me you saved a copy?"

"Sadly, no, my point is I didn't dream of Fairy tale weddings and there weren't any princes in my neighborhood growing up."

"So, you'd elope?"

"I said if I was marrying Race Johnson, I'd elope and save the aggravation of wedding crashers. Didn't a helicopter crash at Austin and Sydney's wedding?"

"You have a point."

22

"The sign says 'Closed'," Baylor called as Joey joined her at the entrance of a high-end furniture store. "It is Sunday."

"It's closed for us. Let me tell Amber we are out front."

"They closed the store for you?"

"And the others, we all need to finish the houses we picked. We also have a Guest house and a studio. This store is going to do quite well with just us here."

"I'll bet. Will you all be needing any Antique books to fill your shelves once you buy them?" Baylor teased.

"I might need a few. You see, my girlfriend loves books," Joey said, kissing Baylor in a not fit for public sort of kiss.

"I called it. Race owes me ten bucks," Griff laughed, opening the door with the help of one of the sales people.

"Griff, you know you cheated. Our Mom called ahead. Nice to see you, Baylor."

"You too, Finley."

"Just get inside, we have shopping to do," Griff rolled his eyes.

"You don't seem thrilled," Baylor said, feeling like she was a part of the group instantly.

"We have a difference of opinion on some things."

"A Pool table in the center of the main room is a huge no. There's a Rec room and a basement. You can put your games there," Finley giggled.

"Fine, I will let you have your way."

"I could just live elsewhere."

"No! I'm sorry. I was joking. I love you. I love real furniture," Griff back-peddled.

"They are basically large children," Teagan laughed as Race and Griff jumped on one of the beds.

"I'm thinking about getting a trampoline for the backyard," Finley agreed.

"Baylor, come look at this," Joey called from across the expansive room, where one of the Sales people was clearly focused on him.

"Time to save my brother from the Sales woman trying to give him her number," Finley smiled

"Is that my job now, to run interference?" Baylor asked with a grin

"That depends. Are you two official or just seeing each other?" Teagan inquired.

"I'm not sure what constitutes official, but he keeps saying that our first date was his last first date. That sounds serious, but he could be joking."

"He's not joking, Baylor. Joey doesn't tell women what they want to hear. He means it."

"Alright, then I will make sure the Sales woman knows he's not available." Baylor liked that the other women were treating her like she belonged.

"This one or this one?" Joey said, pointing to two different sectional sofas.

"The leather one," Baylor answered.

"We will take that one. Bay, do you think we need a chair or two to match?"

It didn't go unnoticed that he kept saying *"we"* instead of "I".

"Yes, but not leather, that would be overkill. A pair of overstuffed chairs for near the fireplace."

"Do you have a preferred color?" the Sales person asked, sounding annoyed that she was no longer getting Joey's attention.

"Bay?"

Baylor was not sure it was her place to pick out the fine details of Joey's décor, but she wasn't going to let the woman know that.

"Brick red, with a deep beige accent rug against the lighter wood of the floors."

"Perfect, let's look at rugs," Joey reached out, taking her hand.

"I just ruined that woman's day," Baylor whispered.

"I'm sorry about that," Joey looked guilty.

"Joey, I know who you are. I know people assume we are together, but they still aren't sure. One of the associates was flirting with Austin and he's married. I fully expect women to keep trying. As long as you're not tempted, we will be fine."

"I'm done, stick a fork in me. You are my endgame."

"That's nice to hear, but it is still early. We barely know each other. I'm optimistic or I wouldn't have agreed to that first date. I just need you to promise one thing."

"Anything."

"If you ever decide to take a woman up on what she's offering, call me and let me go first, close our door before opening another."

"That's fair, but I'm not going to ever make that call. I can't explain it, Baylor, but I think I've been waiting for you."

"You're good with the words, Joey, but you are still human."

"Then, you need to come on tour when we go back out."

"One day at a time, Joey, I'm already picking out furniture for a man I've been on one date with."

"This counts as date two, maybe three. Dinner will be at least four, then there is tomorrow."

"Tomorrow, I have to work. I do have a business I've been neglecting."

"How will I know where to put all this furniture when it's delivered tomorrow?"

"You are a big boy. You will do fine. It's your house, Joey, not mine."

"Someday, when you move in, I want you to feel at home."

"You're moving me in now?"

"I already sort of proposed."

"No, we just talked about my idea of a perfect wedding."

"Baylor, I have never asked a girl what their perfect wedding would be. I have never cared. Since I fully intend for your wedding to be mine as well, I was curious."

"I think, maybe, I'd need to think about that for a while, maybe go on a few more dates to make sure you don't change your mind."

"What about you? Are you going to change your mind about me?"

"I'm just trying to catch up. You move fast. That's not a complaint. I'm just not used to men who talk about the future right away."

"You and I, what we have, is different. I know it, you know it, or you wouldn't still be here with me, picking out furniture for your possible future home."

"You're right."

"You came to the concert despite feeling like something could go wrong. What's you're feeling about us?"

"I'm cautiously optimistic. It all sounds too good to be true. I appreciate your honesty and your clear intentions, I do. I feel like everyone here already assumes I'm sticking around for a while."

"Just a while? My mother called Finley the second we left. She's already thinking of you as family."

"I like your family."

"And they love you. Now, which rug do you think for in front of the fireplace?"

"That depends. Are we getting a dog?" Baylor smirked, playing along. She had no intentions of moving in with Joey until they were well established and maybe engaged. Her outlook had changed from days ago, when she wasn't sure he was really interested in her. Joey White was most definitely serious about her.

"Do you want a dog? It would have to be a small one because of the bus when we are on tour."

"I was kidding. I like dogs, but it's a little early for co-parenting a pet."

"Then, why did you ask?"

"I was thinking about the color. Pet stains are hard to get out and these rugs are expensive."

"If our imaginary dog soils the rug, I will buy a new one."

"Alright, then this one," Baylor pointed to a light beige rug with a swirling mauve pattern running through it.

23

"They have decided your girl's attacker can stand trial," Mark told Joey when he returned from dropping Baylor off at work that day.

In the last week, he had spent more time with the woman that he had spotted in the crowd. She was more than he could have hoped for. She didn't care about his money and, so far, his fame had caused more trouble for her.

"I'll call Baylor and let her know."

"Amber is calling her. This is a good thing, Joey. She needs to pay for what she did. She attacked Baylor and all of the people interviewed said it was unprovoked. Baylor just asked what the woman's problem was."

"That doesn't sound like a sane person's reaction."

"If she had been declared unfit, she could spend a couple of months in a facility then be released without answering to the charges. At least. she will be charged with an assault. The fact that she bit Rufus as well should give her a long time to think about what she did. Baylor needs to get a Restraining Order."

"They let her out?"

"She made bail."

"When is this trial?"

"Next week, they moved it up because of the publicity."

"Oh good, so Baylor will have to testify and the entire thing will turn into a circus. She's going to want to run far from all of this when the media gets through with her."

"She's tough. I'm glad to see how much you care for her."

"I care for a lot of people."

"True, but there's a difference between caring for a fan that gets hurt and caring for a woman you love. You love her. It shows. I've watched all of you fall, but this is unexpected."

"Why is it so hard for you to understand? I found the one. I don't know how I knew, but I knew the moment I saw her in the front row."

"I've seen the tapes. It was like something clicked. Race jumping to rescue a woman, even Austin, would have made sense. All of you are kind-hearted. It was the way you carried her off. I really thought you knew her."

"So did millions of fans."

"And one angry woman, I mean, who bites a man after shoving a stranger into a stage? I'm surprised they said she was fit to stand trial."

"I want her behind bars."

"I think that is likely, but you never know."

"I'm going to suggest she move in with me to be safe."

"I thought she already had," Mark chuckled.

"No, she stayed here last night and I was at her place the day before. We are alternating."

"You haven't slept apart for nearly a week and a half. When you commit, you commit. "

"Yes, I do."

"I'm happy for you. Now, go practice. Austin wrote a new song, I hear."

"The kid's not even here and he's already writing love songs to the unborn."

"Anything that keeps him writing," Mark said, walking with Joey to the home they converted to a studio. Mark and Amber had decided to take the other house instead of it being a Guest house. The neighborhood was now one big happy family.

"I was thinking," Joey said, walking down the pristine sidewalk.

"Yes."

"The island of land in the turnaround, it would make a nice park for the kids."

"Kids?" Mark smiled.

"Oh please, we all know that you and Amber are either pregnant or trying. It's about time. How did Sydney and Austin beat you to it?"

"It will make a really nice park within view of all of the houses, good idea."

"No comment on the pregnant or trying thing?"

"No comment," Mark laughed.

"There he is. It's about time. You can't just suck face with your girlfriend all day," Griff taunted."

"I recall you sucking face with my sister practically every time I turned around."

"That was intentional."

"Asshole."

"I love you two like brothers. Speaking of brothers, will you be my best man?"

"Me, not Race?"

"Here's the thing. Race needs a best man too. The girls want us to both get married on the same day, something small, simple, just family."

"Like the small, simple Family wedding on an island during a hurricane."

"It was a tropical storm that was not in the forecast for that week," Austin called, setting up the last of the mics in the practice space.

"I will be your best man. Assume Race had first pick and chose Austin."

"I'm marrying your sister. It seemed only right I ask you."

"I'll take that as a yes. When is this small, dual wedding and where?"

"It's in two weeks, here."

"Excuse me?"

"Why wait? We are already living together. Your Mom asked me when I was going to make an honest woman out of her daughter."

"She was kidding. You do know that?"

"I do, but I want Finley to be mine officially."

"Do I need a shotgun for this wedding? I was just talking about babies with Mark."

"Mark, you and Amber are expecting?"

"No comment, he was suggesting the island be made into a park. That's what brought up the subject of children."

"Good call, I love that idea. There is no shotgun needed, not for the lack of me trying."

"Griff, that's my sister. I don't want to hear about you trying."

"You should call her. She wanted to see if it was alright if she asked Baylor to be her Maid of Honor."

"Why wouldn't it be alright?"

"Because you have never been in a relationship this long."

"If it wouldn't terrify Baylor, I'd suggest a three-couple ceremony. She doesn't buy into the Fairy tale Wedding thing."

"You two have discussed this?"

"I sort of brought it up on our first date."

"If she didn't run, then she might be the one."

"She is the one, so text Finley and tell her to go ahead and ask."

24

"This is our three-week anniversary," Joey said, handing Baylor a big box.

"What is this?"

"A gift for you."

"I didn't get you anything."

"Yes, you did. You got me the best girlfriend a guy could ask for. The box isn't really from me. Finley sent it."

"You are crazy. Get in here before someone sees you."

"Who is looking at this car and thinking I'm in it? That s the point of owning this classic."

"Oh, so now it's a classic?"

"It is a classic. A new paint job and it's worth a lot. I keep the exterior looking like I bought it at the junkyard so no one notices me"

"Genius plan, until you get out of the car." Baylor reached up, giving him a kiss as the door shut behind him.

"Are you doing anything two weeks from now?"

"What's two weeks from now?" Baylor asked, liking the fact that Joey was planning ahead. She had stopped worrying about when he would move on. For a guy that never really had a girlfriend, he was really good at being a boyfriend.

"Open the box and see."

"Oh?"

"Just open it. It's sort of time sensitive."

Baylor opened the box and saw a beautiful basket filled with lotions and soaps."

"What is this?" Baylor looked confused.

"Read the card."

The card read:

Will you be my Maid of Honor?

' The card also included a date, only two weeks away.

"This has to be a mistake."

"Why would you think that?"

"Well, for one, I've known her for the same three weeks I've known you. She has Sydney and Teagen, who are more like family than friends. I'm sure she has a lot of choices. Maid of Honor is a big deal. She must have mixed up the boxes."

"No mix up, she wants you to be her Maid of Honor. Teagan isn't available, since she's getting married to Race at the same time, and Sydney is her Matron of Honor."

"She has to have friends, other family."

"Baylor, if you don't want to say yes, then don't say yes."

"I'm just trying to figure out why she would choose me?"

"She likes you. My family loves everything about you, including me." Baylor's heart pounded in her chest. This was the closest Joey had come to the actual "L" word.

"I love all of you too."

"Then, say yes. The wedding is small and kind of a secret. The press is bound to get wind of it when you all go dress shopping."

"Just when they stopped staking out the store," Baylor joked.

"I know that the press, and the fans, and the invasion of your personal life is hard on you. If I were a better man, I'd leave you to your calm, quiet life."

"You are the best man I know, Joey."

"I come with major baggage. The press hounding you, making things up when the story is too boring. I know you haven't really taken me seriously when I said you were my last first date, but every day, I am more convinced that you are meant to be mine."

"I can't argue that, Joey. I am alright with the baggage if it means I have you."

"Is that a yes? Finley asked me to call right away when I got your answer. She was going come herself, but I wanted to see you and maybe get invited to spend the night."

"Joey, you don't need an invitation to stay. We haven't slept apart since that first night."

"The plan is that we never sleep apart again," Joey said with conviction.

"I still worry you will get sick of me. You'll go on tour and then what?"

"And I hope that by then, you will have agreed to come with me. Barbara can run the store. You can do all the Online sales on the road."

"You go on tour in five months. Ask me again in three."

"I will be asking, Baylor."

"I hope so. Let's call Finley, then I'll make you dinner."

"I love that you can cook."

"Don't get it in your head that I'm going to do that all the time."

"When I convince you that I'm not going anywhere and that you should move in with me, I will hire a cook if you want."

"If you convince me, and if I decide to leave this luxurious apartment, then I would rather have a cleaning lady once a week. Your house is not something I want to clean."

"A cleaning lady?"

"An older lady, maybe one with grandchildren," Baylor smiled.

"You think I'd cheat on you with the cleaning lady?"

"No but just to be safe," Baylor closed the space between them and kissed Joey. The kiss meant to be playful soon turned serious.

"I'm not hungry right now, are you?" she asked panting. She was so worked up she was ready to strip down in the Living room. She would have if the curtain in that room hadn't been so sheer."

"I'm hungry alright, but not for food. I can't get enough of you, Baylor. "

"The feeling is entirely mutual."

The two made it to Baylor's bedroom, still kissing like a couple of teens. Joey White was addictive. Baylor wanted to believe all of the promises and declarations he made to her. He wasn't trying to deceive her, but a man like Joey was hard to hold onto. He was swarmed weekly, sometimes daily, by woman who would do anything for even a moment's attention from him.

Her heart was completely in love with Joey and her head was finding it hard to argue that it was too soon.

She was either going to have this man forever or go down in flames. In that moment, with him pressed against her, she knew that taking the risk was well worth it.

25

"I am driving you to meet the girls," Joey grinned as Baylor opened the back door of her bookstore. She had expected one of the guards to be picking her up that morning.

"I thought you were at the Court house, giving your statement to the judge."

Joey and Baylor weren't going to be required to show up when Sue, the pushy biter, was tried. The disruption Joey and his association Baylor would cause was something the Judge wanted to avoid. The woman had waved the right to a Public trial. She was, apparently, getting backlash, and not in a good way, for hurting Joey White's girlfriend without provocation.

"I went to the Court house, explained what I saw, and how I reacted. It's really not necessary, since the entire thing is on tape."

"Not to mention, a hundred videos taken with your fans' phones and made into Gifs."

"I'm not sure if the one with you face-planting on the edge of the stage will ever go away."

"Now that my head is healed, I can see the humor in it."

"Did you give your statement?"

"Yesterday."

"Rufus will be at the hearing, but I can't see them letting her off easy. She assaulted two people."

"I heard her excuse. She said she thought you were looking at her and I was blocking your view."

"I am surprised they didn't declare her unfit. She had to be crazy to bite Rufus."

"I agree the man is a monster."

"I need to warn you," Joey said as they pulled his car out of the back alley behind her store.

"Sounds serious."

"I don't think so, but you might. Yasmine will be with you ladies at the shop."

"Yasmine, your Ex?"

"Sort of, we both agreed it was a disaster and she's dating a roadie. I hear they are serious."

"You're worried I'll be jealous?"

"Maybe?" Joey shrugged. "I just thought it might be awkward."

"Do you love her?"

"No, not like that, she's a good friend that been with us for years."

"Then, I look forward to meeting her."

"Thank you."

"What are you thanking me for?"

"For being you. I knew the moment I saw you that my life was about to change for the better."

"Are you sure you weren't looking for our friend Suezilla?"

"I am sure," Joey laughed as he pulled up to a small shop that Baylor had never even noticed. It was on the second floor of a laundromat and only the sign on the door indicated what was upstairs.

"I will come and get you when you're finished."

"I'm sure I can get a ride if you are busy."

"We are practicing for a few hours, but I think this might take that long. Call me when you are done. We are staying at my place tonight, am I right?"

"Joey, we stay there almost every night. Half of my things are already in your closet."

"I'll take that as a yes."

"Yes."

Joey's phone rang and Finley's name came up on the Caller ID. He answered. The smirk on his face told Baylor he knew exactly what his sister was about to say.

"Griff called. You are late. You need to let Baylor breathe or you will smother her. We are all here already. Let the woman come have a Girl's afternoon," Finely scolded.

"I will see you later," Baylor laughed, climbing out of the car after a quick kiss.

"Call me."

"Maybe, I'll just show up. The Guard at your gate loves me."

"He's fired," Joey barked.

"Stop, I'll see you later. Have a good practice."

Baylor rushed up the stairs. She didn't like being late and inconveniencing people. She already was nervous to meet Yasmine. The woman was Joey's Ex but, more than that, she was a friend. The Rascal crew and staff, along with the band, was a tightknit group. She was starting to think she might be with this man for the long haul. It was dangerous to hope, but she couldn't help it. With babies on the way and a double wedding she was part of, it was hard for her to avoid thinking about the future.

"There she is. I thought he would never let you get out of the car," Joey's mother met her at the top of the stairs. His mother was there. Of course, she was also Finley's mother, so Baylor should have realized she would be at her daughter's side, picking out Wedding dresses.

"Nice to see you, Mrs. ..."

"Jane, you call me Jane for now."

"For now?"

"With all of this Wedding talk and the way my son is with you, I think maybe, one day, you will call me Mom."

"That's very nice of you, Jane."

"It's in the eyes, you know."

"What's in the eyes."

"Love, he loves you."

"Oh, I don't think we are quite there yet."

"It's just a matter of time. Come, we are having a Fashion show. Teagan and Finley have both picked out three dresses. We are the final judges. Have you met Olivia?"

"Yes, I have. She and Rufus rescued me from an impromptu mob at my shop."

"And Yasmine?"

"I look forward to meeting her."

"Then, let's introduce you," Jane said with a smile, taking her hand.

Baylor had never seen anything like shopping with these women. When money is no object, it's easy to find the right dress. At least, that's what Baylor had thought going in. Both Finley and Teagan had come from families that were far from rich, so they had a limit set and they stuck to it.

Baylor was sure the Shopkeeper, who was also the Seamstress, would have liked them to pick something more expensive, since most Sales people worked on commission.

"The dresses are stunning. Be prepared for an onslaught of interest. The wedding is private, but we will be posting pictures and giving you credit as the Designer."

"Oh, that's right. I could give them to you," the woman said, realizing that her tiny shop was now going to be the go-to Wedding shop in the area after this.

"Absolutely not! You are already charging too little for your beautiful dresses," Teagan insisted.

"Thank you," the woman blushed.

26

As the group of women dispersed several hours later, Rufus came for Olivia, Teagan, and Sydney. Sydney had an appointment with the Doctor and Teagan was tagging along.

"Is she really tagging along to Sydney's appointment and bringing her Aunt with her?" Baylor said out loud.

"I think that Sydney might be introducing her to her OBGYN."

"Is she...?" Baylor asked Finley.

"If I had to guess, yes."

"Is that why the weddings are so soon?"

"Oh please, it's the 21st Century," Yasmine chuckled. "I think both Fin here and Teagan want it to be official. Being a Rock Star's wife has its advantages."

"Like?" Baylor hadn't spoken to Yasmine much, but she seemed nice.

"Like the women don't chase married men as hard as the unmarried ones. The fans figure that just because they have a girlfriend doesn't mean they wouldn't be interested in a little fun or more."

"And a Wedding ceremony changes that?" Baylor didn't dispute Yasmine's reasoning. Joey got far more attention than the other three and two were only engaged.

"No, it just weeds out the women that want a little fun. The ones that want more will try."

"Is that why you two broke up?"

"I wasn't sure if he had mentioned me."

"He did."

"That's a good sign."

"It is?"

"Yes, if he didn't see you as long-term, he wouldn't have bothered. So far, you are the longest he has been with any woman, with no sign of that changing. To answer your question. no, I knew that some women would lie, steal, and claim they had already been with Joey, if they thought it would work. We just didn't fit."

"That's what he said."

"Joey doesn't really lie. If he says something, he means it. I had a crush on him for years. When he finally noticed me, it wasn't what I expected."

"What did you expect?"

"A spark, a connection, I love Joey, but I was looking for a soulmate, not a playmate."

"I get that."

"This might be none of my business, but do you love him?"

"Good question. I do love him. I'm just hoping he feels the same."

"He does. You are together nearly a month and you are his sister's Maid of Honor. His Mother loves you. It's a matter of time before he askes you to move in with him."

"He already did, kind of."

"And are you moving?"

"He's talked about being on the road and selling my books online. I know my Assistant would do a great job running the shop and she could save on rent if I just gave her my apartment."

"I have known him a long time, Baylor. From what I see and what I've heard, you are it for him. He told Griff that he found his one. If you repeat that, I will deny it," Yasmine smiled.

"Thank you, that helps. I feel like he loves me, but he hasn't said the words."

"Words are cheap. Its actions that show you what a man truly feels." Yasmine's phone pinged and she read the message, looking back up at Baylor when she finished. "The boys are running overtime at practice. Rufus has asked that I drop you off. Are you comfortable with that, or I can call one of the other Security people?"

"I like you, Yasmine. This isn't High school. You dated the man I am currently dating. I am mature enough to except that you are friends now. I think that's nice. I don't talk to anyone I used to date and some were not all bad."

"Then, let's head out. Which home are you two sleeping at tonight?"

"You know about that?" Baylor started to blush.

"Baylor, you have a Security person on duty at all times. The woman that hurt you is out on bail and she's not the only nut that thinks you are stealing Joey."

"I didn't know she was out on bail," Baylor said nervously

"It would be stupid for her to even leave her home, but until she is sentenced, you have a shadow."

"I'm okay with that. Can we stop by my place first? I could just have Joey come when he is done."

"I hear you own a bookstore."

"It's mostly Antique and Tare editions, but we do have a Romance and Mystery section that most people enjoy."

"Who doesn't enjoy a good romance?"

Yasmine drove to Baylor's and wandered around the store while Baylor packed a bag. The apartment no longer seemed like home. It seemed like a place to sleep and keep her things, but not home. Home was where Joey was. Baylor had time to decide what to do when he had to go on tour. He was right. She could do everything online.

She barely had any clothing left at her place. It was maybe time to decide to take the leap or play it safe. The only one questioning the longevity of their relationship was her, apparently. Even the Ex-girlfriend seemed to think Joey was committed to her.

"I am ready," she said, tossing the bag she had packed over her shoulder. "Barbara, I'll be in in the morning."

"No need, Junie is coming to train with me. She needs an afterschool job and I thought this would be perfect. That's alright, isn't it?"

"Junie is perfect. Thank you."

"I figure when the band goes on tour, I'm going to need all the help I can get."

"Why?"

"Because you, My Dear, will be going with them. I can't imagine that man leaving you behind," Barbara smiled.

"No comment," Baylor said, having no reason to disagree.

"She's right, you know," Yasmine said as soon as they were back in the car.

"Who, Barbara?"

"Yes, I don't see Joey leaving you behind either. I like the idea too. You are good people. I think we can be friends."

"I think we definitely can." Baylor felt a weird sense of relief. She hadn't made any lifelong decisions just yet, but she was leaning in that direction.

27

"Wasn't that the turn off?" Baylor looked to Yasmine.

"It was, but we have a tail."

"A tail, like a person following us?"

"Yes, exactly, so far, the general public doesn't know exactly where their houses are. Since the wedding is there, I'd prefer to lose whoever is following rather than have them stopped at the gate."

"The gate would be a dead giveaway."

"Yes, it would."

"How do they know to follow us?"

"They probably saw us leave your place. Baylor, the world knows who you are. Even if they don't follow the band, they have seen the videos."

"Great, now what?"

"Now, we lose them." Yasmine seemed to be excited by the chase. Baylor was not.

"Should we call someone?" Baylor asked.

"You have Rufus's number?"

"Yes."

"Call him. If you call Joey or the guys, they will worry. Joey might do something stupid."

"Like what."

"Like come to save you."

"You think they are after me."

"Yes, Baylor, Joey and I never went public. It's someone who knew where you lived. They were waiting for a picture or Joey."

"Can you tell who it is?" Baylor craned her neck to look behind them."

"Only that it is a female. There could be someone in the back seat. I can't tell. Hold on."

"Hold on" was the only warning Baylor had before the car was spinning. Yas had executed a full 180 degree turn and they were now headed toward the car that had been following them.

"Yasmine!" Baylor exclaimed, seeing the car that had been following them was now coming straight at them, intentionally crossing the median.

Yasmine stomped on the accelerator trying to get out of the other car's way.

"This is not paparazzi; Did you call Rufus?"

"I texted that we were in trouble. He just responded 'K'."

"Man of few words, that Rufus."

"She was trying to hit us."

"And she almost succeeded. I've pulled that move a hundred times to lose some fan or photographer. They never try to run me off the road after."

"She's back to following."

"I see that. We have to get out of town. She's reckless and could hurt someone."

"She tried to T-bone the car. What fan wants a dead Rock star, what photographer?"

"Remember what happened to Princess Diana?"

"I am not a princess. I'm not a star," Baylor yelled.

"Baylor, I need you to try and stay calm."

"I'm trying."

"I think that the woman in the car might be the woman from the concert."

"She's out on bail? Wasn't someone watching her?"

"Yes, I can't explain how they didn't notice. That's a problem for another time."

"She's not going to give up. Joey and I think she is insane. We were surprised they said she could stand trial."

"A trial would put her away for longer, but it did allow her out on bail before the proceedings."

"She's catching up," Baylor said, twisting to see over the back seat.

"Get down. If it is her, she wants you, not me."

"I think she's seen me by now."

"She could have a weapon. Get down," Yasmine yelled.

Baylor dropped down immediately, hoping that crazy Sue wasn't packing. She was running on pure adrenaline. Her phone pinging was her only distraction.

"Rufus is five minutes away," Baylor read the message aloud.

"Tell him we think it's Sue. Hell, just call him and put it on speaker. He only texted because you did. He thought it wasn't safe to talk."

"Okay," Baylor pushed call.

"Yas, what's the situation?" Rufus even sounded scary over the phone.

Yas rattled off a summery of the last few minutes. Those minutes seemed like an eternity. All Baylor wanted to do was go home. With that thought, she realized she pictured Joey's house in her mind when she thought of home now.

Her apartment was somewhere to live. Joey's place was home.

"Baylor, hold on," Yas said as she disconnected with Rufus in order to concentrate on her job.

"I hate that sentence," Baylor said, grabbing the door handle as the car spun out a right after the car behind made impact.

"What the hell is she doing?" Yasmine said, trying to maneuver around the vehicle that had hit them from behind intentionally. While spinning the wheel to get out of her way, this spin didn't seem as controlled as the last one.

"I think, maybe, she's trying to kill me. When she pushed me, she thought that Joey was looking at her and I was in the way. She even put that in her statement."

"Sure, kill the competition, that seems sane to me," Yas groaned. "We have another problem."

"What now?"

"We are low on gas."

"This kind of shit doesn't happen in the movies," Baylor exclaimed throwing her hands up.

"I can see why Joey loves you," Yas said, laughing hard.

"This isn't funny."

"No, it's not. I'd say we have maybe a mile or two left before we die."

"Don't say die!"

"Right, I meant before the car dies. Here's what I need you to do. We wait in the car until she gets out. I will rush her and you will run."

"Run where?"

"Anywhere away from her."

"What if she has a gun?"

"Unless she's some crack shot, I will shoot first."

"You have a gun!" Baylor was starting to panic.

"It's got rubber bullets in it, but they hurt like hell. They will take her down."

"Okay, I run, you shoot, good plan."

"She's coming around for more. Her driving skills are impressive."

"All the better to kill us with."

"Hold on."

"I'm holding. I never stopped holding." Baylor screamed as the lunatic in the other car rammed them again. This time the spin was out of Yasmine's control altogether. The vehicle lurched to the right then started to roll. Baylor sat up as her side skid into a ditch on the side of the road, watching as Yasmine's side rose into the air.

Baylor fully expected the car to roll, but it didn't. Instead, it came to rest on its side, with her side against the ground and Yasmine falling toward her. The only thing that prevented the Guard from landing on her was the seatbelt holding her suspended in the air.

"You okay?" Yasmine asked.

"Peachy," Baylor groaned, trying to get her belt off.

Yasmine skillfully grabbed the handle above the driver's door while unclipping her seatbelt and then lowering herself until both she and Baylor were standing on the passenger door, looking up at the driver's door.

"New plan, get in back. I'm going out that way. She will expect you to follow. Wait until I yell, then come out the rear driver's side door.

"The doors are feet apart. What difference does it make?"

"It makes one foot difference. If she had a weapon and is aiming for the front door, you will be at the back. You need to trust me."

"You are right. Back door, got it."

Baylor started to squeeze through the space left to her right with the vehicle in this position. She only had to step across to the back, while Yasmine climbed to the driver's door, using the seats as stepping stones.

As the door opened and Yas popped out with all the skill of an Olympic athlete, Baylor wondered if she could hoist herself up and over in time.

28

It was hard to tell what was happening outside. All Baylor could hear was the blood rushing in her ears. Her heart was pounding. She wanted to see Joey. She wanted to tell him she loved him. She was done waiting for him to say it first.

"Go," Yasmine's strained voice echoed.

Baylor had to push the door twice before it opened and stayed open. The first time, she nearly knocked her elf out when the door fell back toward her head. Then, she scrambled to the top, pulling with all her strength to get out, flopping on her stomach and doing a less than graceful roll to get out of the open doorway that was now more of a hatch than a door.

Baylor had to roll out and landed on the ground with a thud before righting herself.

She saw Yasmine had a woman pinned, with her knee pressed into the woman's back and her gun to the woman's head.

The bullets might be rubber and Baylor knew nothing about guns, but she was sure that would kill the woman beneath her.

"Run."

"Still?" Baylor asked, still in shock. The matter looked well at hand.

"Yes, she's strong and I really don't want to kill her. The paperwork would be endless," Yasmine said, making Baylor smile.

She was sure that Yasmine had said that to let the woman know she had the ability to kill her but was choosing not to.

"He is mine," a muffled groan came from the woman below Yasmine's knee.

"You ran two women off the road with intent to harm at least one of us. That's Attempted Murder. We can add that to the Assault charges and I'd say you might see the light of day in your eighties, if you are lucky," Yasmine said with a grin.

Baylor was still unsure whether to run or stay to make sure Yasmine was alright. She seemed very capable. Baylor had no skills, but two against one still seemed a better option.

A car screeched to a halt on the desolate back road Yasmine had led them to in order to avoid others getting hurt by this woman.

Not knowing who was in the car triggered her "fight or flight". The problem was she was still partially in the sandy ditch.

"It's Rufus," Yasmine called as Baylor tried to go around the car to hide.

"Thank god. I'm no runner and I don't know where we are. You'd probably have to send 'Search and Rescue' if I went that way."

"Baylor, get out of there. That car isn't stable," Rufus bellowed and the command seemed urgent.

He was right. The car that had landed on its side was now starting to tilt away from her. Any moment, the thing would roll onto the hood, but that didn't make her safe at all.

In the time it took for her to realize she might still be in trouble. Rufus had run to her and was reaching for her.

He didn't bother waiting for her to reach for him. He grabbed and yanked her the few feet between her and safety as the car creaked and groaned, rolling onto its back and settling in the ditch. The passenger side slid as the car shifted right into the spot she had been standing, but it was now upside-down.

"It looks like a dead cockroach," she said as the vehicle seemed to still be moving in a rocking motion in the sandy cradle of the shallow ditch.

"Are you hurt?" Tegan and Sydney hovered as Baylor just sat down.

"You missed your appointment," Baylor said looking at Teagan."

"There will be other appointments. Do you need an ambulance?"

"For what."

"Your head is bleeding on the right side and you're holding your arm funny."

"Not again," Baylor said, standing and pushing past the two women to where Rufus now had the woman secured.

"You… this is all your fault!" Baylor screamed at her. "The funny part is I didn't even know Joey White. I didn't know any of them. I was there because my friend had free tickets. Because of you, I now have the perfect man and he's mine, Suzie, he's mine. All because you decided that I was a threat. If you had never pushed me, I would have never met the man. Chew on that for the next sixty years."

"Baylor, the police are on their way. Are you sure you don't need the hospital?" Olivia asked, holding her phone.

"No ambulance, if I need a hospital, we can just drive. Ambulances are expensive."

"You are so the right woman for Joey," Yasmine laughed.

"What?"

"Most women wouldn't care about how much something cost when they were dating a very wealthy man like Joey."

"I don't want Joey's money," Baylor looked confused.

"Exactly, you are perfect for him. I also think you are still in shock, so maybe the ambulance isn't necessary, but the hospital might be. I'll call Finley."

"Okay," Baylor agreed.

As soon as Baylor and Yasmine spoke with the police, all of them piled into the SUV that Rufus and Olivia had come in with Teagan and Sydney.

Finley was meeting them at the hospital. Baylor had asked Rufus to wait on calling Joey and interrupting their practice for her.

"It's like déjà vu," Finley said, coming into the private room.

"I don't think it's that bad," Baylor smiled.

"No, it isn't that bad. The ER Doc said you have a tiny laceration over your ear and a dislocated shoulder."

"That is better than I thought it would be when the car went off the road. How is Yasmine?"

"She's fine. She wasn't the one that hit her head on the window. She said her seatbelt saved her from landing on you."

"That would have hurt for sure."

"Are you ready for me to put that arm back in place?"

"Will it hurt?"

"Yes."

"Aren't you supposed to say only a little or not much?"

"You don't lie to family, even a white lie."

"Aren't all of your lies '*White'* lies?" Baylor said cracking herself up.

"They gave her Pain meds," Sydney explained as the others joined in.

"She has a point," Tegan giggled.

While Baylor was distracted, Finley gently took her arm and re-set the shoulder. Baylor's scream only lasted a second before she caught herself.

"You were right. That hurt."

"Feel better now?"

"Yes."

"I recommend a couple of days in a sling and no gymnastics."

"And I was just going to sign up to be the next Olympian. Way to dash a woman's dreams," Baylor giggled.

Finley started to say something, but the door flying open and Joey rushing in, panicked, stopped all the words from coming out."

'Baylor," Joey was actually shaking. The look on his face was a clear sign that this man loved her. He didn't need to say the words. She could feel it.

"I'm fine."

"She is fine. I just re-set her shoulder. Be careful," Finley warned as Joey went to hug her.

"Thank god," Joey said, holding her but being careful. "They need to put that lunatic away and lose the key."

"I think they might after this," Baylor hoped.

"You're coming home with me."

"I was on my way there when this happened. Thanks to Yasmine, I'm in one piece."

"She's the best," Sydney agreed.

"Can we get out of here?" Joey looked at his sister for the answer.

"Yes, I'll get the release papers."

29

"How in the world did they get this all set up on two weeks' notice?" Baylor asked, seeing the set-up for that afternoon's double wedding. It was like a Fairy tale with lights that would be lit later that evening. Waiters and caterers, as well as designers, were putting the final touches on what already looked perfect.

"Money talks," Yasmine smiled. "Shouldn't you be getting dressed?"

"I'm getting my hair done in fifteen minutes. I just wanted to see this. It's so..."

"Over the top?" Yasmine asked.

"No, it's not as over the top as I imagined. It's simple elegance with a bit of romance."

"Have you thought about what your own wedding would look like?"

"Not until recently," Baylor blushed.

"That is just a matter of time. I've known Joey a long time. He's found his person."

"I like that. I don't think I'd go to this extreme. I don't actually care how it looks or where it is. I'm not religious. I only have a few people, other than all of you, that I'd invite. I real don't think I need to worry about that right now. I'm more worried about tripping down that aisle."

"You will do fine."

Baylor didn't feel as out of place as she first thought she would, standing next to Finley as Joey stood with Griff.

The vows were simple, the Officiant letting each of the two couples exchange their own, one at a time.

"Are you crying?" Finley whispered as Teagan and Race exchanged rings and were pronounced Husband and Wife.

"I always cry at weddings. I feel like all of you are family and I have only known you for little over a month."

"I feel like you are family as well. You fit into this crazy group and my brother loves you," she said in a low voice before joining her new husband. They walked back down the aisle, leaving Joey to escort her, while Austin and Sydney followed Race and Teagan.

"I think I like weddings where no helicopter crashes ruin the day," Joey smiled at her and Baylor was done. She was willing to move in and spend as much time as he was willing to give with him. She knew this was too soon. She knew this was not a man that normally stuck with one woman for long. She was actually the longest relationship that he had ever had, other than his band and immediate family.

"Don't tempt fate," Finley hissed from in front of them as they stopped to pose for the photographer they hired.

This event was about to make the man's career, giving him the exclusive. Baylor loved the fact that they chose a local caterer and a freelance photographer, instead of the Hollywood elite that some stars might have used.

The party after was for the friends, family, and business associates that had come to watch the private ceremonies.

The traditional first dance followed by. the Bridal party joining in was the first time Joey and Baylor had a chance to dance.

"You are a surprisingly good dancer."

"You questioned my moves?"

"No, I like all of your moves. believe me," Baylor blushed.

"I sure hope so. Guys, can I have the floor?" Joey said when they stopped between songs.

"What are you doing?"

"You will see." Joey's eyes sparked and his smile widened.

"Nearly six weeks ago, I was on stage with these boneheads, playing our final gig of the tour. I spotted a woman in the front row standing next to a woman in a fire engine red bra. The bra was not what caught my eye. It was the woman to her left."

"Joey?" Baylor hissed as she grew redder.

"I'm not done," he grinned. "I knew that with the VIP pass she wore, that I would get a chance to meet her. Little did I l know how apparent my fascination was. I regret her being injured. I regret her being the target of a woman who hurt her not once, but twice. I do not regret that she fell, literally, into my life."

"Since Race had the nerve to get down on one knee at Syd and Austin's wedding, I thought it might be okay if I did the same here."

"Now? Here?" Baylor gasped as Joey fell to one knee, reaching out to show her the most beautiful ring she had ever seen.

"Baylor, I knew the moment I saw you that you were meant to be mine. I know you had a hard time believing that, but when you know, you know. Would you please say yes?"

"You forgot the question," Jane, Joey's Mother yelled, breaking the tension.

"Will you marry me and spend the rest of your life with me? Will you come on tour, because I don't think I could leave you behind? I want to have babies with you, grow old with you."

"Yes," Baylor said, putting him out of his misery.

"To all of it?" Joey looked up soulfully.

"Yes, all of it."

"Thank god," he sighed.

The ring was a sure sign that she had made the right decision. He knew her. The diamond wasn't some huge chunk of "*Look at me*". It was simple and understated elegance.

Wrapping her arms around his neck, they continued to dance slowly to the slow song Baylor knew was a love song that Austin had written with Sydney in mind.

"I think I need to call Maren," Baylor muttered softly.

"To thank her for bringing you to the concert?"

"Yes, that, and I'm going to need a Maid of Honor. Your sister is a married woman now, so she can be my Matron of Honor."

"Matron, uggh, what a terrible word," Finley groaned from behind them.

"It is pretty bad, isn't it?" Baylor laughed.

"I would be honored to be your Matron of Honor, despite my objection to the word. You make my brother happy and you are clearly far too good for him."

"Hey!"

"Oh please, Joey, it's not like you don't know how lucky you are that she said yes."

"I do know that. I love you, Baylor." It was the first time he had ever actually said the words.

"I love you too, Joey White."

If you enjoyed reading Joey and Baylor's story, please consider leaving a review? Reviews are the life's blood of the independent author.

Touching Bass is Book 4, the last in my On Tour series.

I appreciate all of my readers and would love to hear your opinions, good or bad. All suggestions are welcome. You can find me on my Facebook page, Paranormal Twist, for information and updates and to see what's next

Other series by Lynn Leite:
Moon Valley shifters
Pack
On Tour (Contemporary Romance)
Dragon Fire
Undying
Ridgeland Bears
Howlin Ranch
Shifted
Bitten
Ascension
Spark
Omega
Sierra Moon

You can find these and other stand-alone books on Amazon. As always, thank you for reading. Your ratings and comments are much appreciated.

Happy reading, Lynn Leite.

www.ingramcontent.com/pod-product-compliance
Lightning Source LLC
La Vergne TN
LVHW050543160826
845677LV00011B/2162